BABYSITTING NIGHTMARES
THE PHANTOM HOUR

KAT SHEPHERD

ILLUSTRATED BY RAYANNE VIEIRA

[Imprint]
MAKE YOUR MARK

New York

[Imprint]
MAKE YOUR MARK

A part of Macmillan Publishing Group, LLC
175 Fifth Avenue, New York, NY 10010

BABYSITTING NIGHTMARES: THE PHANTOM HOUR. Text copyright © 2019 by Katrina Knudson. Illustrations copyright © 2019 by Imprint. All rights reserved. Printed in the United States of America by LSC Communications, Harrisonburg, Virginia.

Library of Congress Control Number: 2018944957

ISBN 978-1-250-15699-0 (hardcover) / ISBN 978-1-250-15700-3 (ebook)

Our books may be purchased in bulk for promotional, educational, or business use. Please contact your local bookseller or the Macmillan Corporate and Premium Sales Department at (800) 221-7945 ext. 5442 or by email at MacmillanSpecialMarkets@macmillan.com.

Book design by Eileen Savage

Imprint logo designed by Amanda Spielman

Illustrated by Rayanne Vieira

First edition, 2019

1 3 5 7 9 10 8 6 4 2

mackids.com

Steal this book and you will find
A spectre dark will shade your mind
Icy-fingered wraiths will creep
To where you lie in troubled sleep
So take this tome with our fair warning
Lest you join their ranks by morning.

THIS BOOK IS FOR THE WOMEN IN MY FAMILY
AND FOR ALL THOSE WHO CARRY OUR STORIES
AND BRING THEM INTO THE LIGHT

PROLOGUE

THE OLD DOG lay on his back, his long legs poking limply in the air. He snored, wheezing, and his paws twitched gently in the moonlight that spilled across the empty room. From the hallway, a clock somberly chimed the hour, its tones echoing through the sleeping house like funeral bells. The dog's eyelids fluttered, and he let out a low whine. His lip curled, and he shuddered, kicking his back legs until he woke with a muffled yelp. He rolled to his side, panting, the whites of his eyes stark against the shaggy gray of his face.

The dog stood and shook himself, tags jingling. He sniffed the air and then grew still, listening. After a moment, he turned and crossed the dark house, folding his bony body through the dog door. He slouched down the sagging back steps and across the overgrown lawn. A small animal rustled in the long grass, but the old sight hound continued by without a glance. He passed the small pond and the crumbling folly beside it, never stopping until he reached the copse of firs at the edge of the property.

Beneath the dark trees, he picked his way between broken chunks of marble and touched his black nose to the loamy earth. The breeze stirred the branches above him; he lifted his head, and his ears twitched again. Then he bent his head back toward the earth and began to dig.

Hours later, in the cold, gray early morning light, the slope-backed old hound returned limping up the hill, his legs and muzzle coated with heavy, dark soil. Panting, he pushed wearily through the dog door and shuffled across the kitchen, leaving muddy, blood-spattered tracks across the tile floor.

The dog followed the sound of the ticking grandfather clock in the front hall, creeping forward until he stood before it, cowering like a supplicant. With a low whine, he pawed at the glass-fronted door of the clock's cabinet until it opened, his torn claws streaking the glass with a smear of blood.

Something dropped from his mouth, thin and white like a bleached twig. It rattled to the cabinet's bottom, disappearing into its shadowy recesses. The clock's chimes sounded the hour, and the dog retreated, whining and cringing his way back to the comfort of the kitchen.

He stopped at his water dish and drank deeply, draining the bowl before collapsing exhausted into his bed. Through the window, the first light of dawn crept over the horizon.

CHAPTER
1

CLIO CARTER-PETERSON LOOKED in the mirror and gelled the last of her edges back into place before fluffing the bun on top of her head and closing her locker. "You guys good to go?" She slipped on an embroidered jean jacket and scooped her multi-colored patchwork backpack off the floor.

"Do you really have to ask?" Rebecca Chin was already zipped into her cropped bomber jacket, her olive wrists peeping out of its pushed-up sleeves. With her caramel leather backpack firmly strapped over both shoulders and her padded moto-style leggings, she looked ready for action. She bounced impatiently, leather studded high-tops flexing as her heels rose and fell. Tanya Martinez stood beside her, leaning against the lockers with her nose buried in a book. One tawny knee poked out of a hole in her threadbare skinny jeans, and she idly scratched it as she read.

"Sorry; I'm just looking for my history book." Maggie Anderson stood in front of her open locker, sifting through an untidy pile of folders, crumpled papers, and books, her freckled cheeks flushed pink with effort. She brightened as her hand curled around a small hardback. "Oh, hey!"

Tanya looked up. "You found it?"

"Not yet, but here's an overdue library book I lost last month."

Clio reached into her backpack and handed her history book to Maggie. "Here. You can borrow mine. I finished my homework in study hall."

Maggie smiled. "Thanks." She tucked the book into her glittery pink backpack. "Okay. Who's ready for a walk in the woods?"

They headed out of the middle school and over to the parking lot where Clio's aunt, Kawanna Carter, stood waiting for them by her vintage turquoise 1962 Scout. Kawanna's long dreadlocks were pulled back from her smiling coppery brown face, and she wore a knee-length black dress with printed skeletons dancing around the hem. "Thanks for the ride," Clio said, giving her aunt a hug.

Kawanna kissed Clio's forehead. "Anything for my favorite niece and her friends!"

"Auntie, I'm your only niece."

"Doesn't make it any less true," Kawanna said. The girls tossed their backpacks into the covered flatbed and squeezed into the bench seats.

"How did it go at the shop today?" Clio asked. Her aunt had recently moved to Piper, Oregon, and opened Creature Features, a costume and curio shop on Coffin Street. It was a regular hangout spot for the girls, and Clio sometimes helped her aunt behind the counter when the store got busy.

"Now that Halloween's just around the corner, business is really starting to pick up. Any chance you could help out after school this week?"

"I'm babysitting for that new family tomorrow, but maybe later in the week."

"Oh, are they the ones who moved into the old Plunkett Mansion?" Rebecca asked Clio. "I've always wondered what that place was like. Have you been inside yet?"

"Not yet," Clio said. "I'm dying to check it out! I love old places like that; they're like postcards from the past. And the family seemed really nice on the phone."

"We like nice. Nice is good," Maggie said. She poked the back of Clio's seat. "Let's just hope they stay nice and don't get all spooky-weird on you!"

Clio turned around in her seat. "Don't even try to joke about that! I've had enough supernatural experiences, thanks."

"Tell me about it! Never. Again." Rebecca laughed nervously. "The last time anything got 'spooky-weird,' my favorite baby in the world almost ended up trapped in another dimension with an evil Night Queen. I don't even like *thinking* about it!"

Tanya picked at the knee of her jeans. "Oh, I don't know. I mean, it does open up a whole world of scientific inquiry. Aren't you just a little bit curious to know more?"

"Not a chance!" Clio said, and the other girls

laughed. "I liked it a whole lot better when I thought it was just made-up. One visit to the Nightmare Realm was more than enough for me! I feel like I'm still looking over my shoulder, expecting to see the Night Queen and her disgusting spider hair, standing right behind me."

Kawanna pulled the Scout over to the side of a quiet country road and turned off the engine. As Rebecca, Tanya, and Maggie climbed out of the car, Kawanna put her hand on Clio's arm. "Are you sure you don't want me to walk to the clearing with you girls? I know that adults can't see all this supernatural stuff, so I won't be much help, but at least I could keep you company."

Clio shook her head. "Thanks, Auntie, but I think we'll have better luck if we go by ourselves. See you in about an hour."

Kawanna reached for the knit tote bag at her feet and pulled out a Stephen King novel with a snarling dog on the cover. "All right, well, this *Cujo* book and I will be waiting for you right here when you get back." As Clio and her friends started walking down the path into the woods, Kawanna called after her. "Oh, and Li'l Bit?"

Clio stopped and turned. "Yeah?"

Kawanna's expression was serious. "Be careful."

. . . . .

A short time later, Clio found herself looking doubtfully at a pool of blood at her feet. "Are you sure this is going to work?" she asked. She bent down and poked at the Styrofoam tray.

Tanya barely raised her brown eyes from the pages of the large book that lay open in her lap. "This is exactly what it says in the book:

With iron shoe and whitest rose,

Blood and salt,

The door shall close."

The girls stood at the center of a forest clearing. A gnarled old tree loomed over them; the brook between its twisted roots burbled softly. The late afternoon sun gave the surrounding trees' autumn leaves a rich, russet glow, but the chill in the air reminded Clio and her friends that they had little time to waste. Inside the tree's hollow was the entrance to the Nightmare Realm, which would open again during the next full moon unless the girls did something to seal it.

"You brought the old horseshoe from the back

of your aunt's shop, right?" Tanya asked. "Rebecca has the salt. I clipped a rose from my dad's garden, and Maggie handled the blood. If we want to seal the portal and keep out the Night Queen and her minions for good, then this is the way to do it."

"Yeah, but I'm not sure hamburger blood is what the book had in mind," Clio said. "This is just leftovers from Maggie's family barbecue. Maybe the book means . . . I don't know, like . . . *blood* blood."

Maggie tossed her red curls over her shoulder. "Look, the book just said blood, okay? It didn't say what kind. And besides, where else was I supposed to get some? There's tons of blood in meat, anyway. I don't see why it won't work."

Tanya's lip curled. "Eww. I'm so glad I'm a vegetarian."

Clio toyed with a silver ring on her finger and looked at the dark hollow in the base of the tree. "You don't think we should maybe use some of our own? Like cut our hands or something? Just in case?"

"No way," Maggie said. "I barely even let the doctor give me a shot. I'm not about to cut my finger in the middle of the woods."

Clio pulled a bundle of creamy linen from her

backpack and unwrapped a rusted horseshoe. "It's just, you know, I want to remind everybody that we're talking about an open portal to the Nightmare Realm, remember? That place where a bunch of rotting, undead *lusus naturae* live with their queen who swore eternal revenge on us? Don't we all just want to be sure that whatever we do to close that portal will actually *work*, here?"

Rebecca pushed her chestnut bangs out of her eyes and reached into her backpack. "It has to work. We have everything in the recipe. All we need to do is put it all together, right?"

Maggie grinned. "Leave it to you to call it a recipe, Becks."

Rebecca shrugged and held up a dark blue box in one hand and a small glass jar in the other. "I have sea salt and kosher. Which should we use?"

"I say we use both," Clio said. "We don't want to take any chances." She carried the horseshoe over to a flat, mossy patch of earth between two large tree roots. "Let's do it over here so nothing spills."

"I'll grab the bowl I brought." Tanya stood up and picked her way around the roots of a massive yew tree to retrieve a dark wooden salad bowl with a small crack running along the side.

Tanya placed the bowl on the ground and wedged a circle of rocks around the base to keep it steady. Clio laid the horseshoe at the bottom of the bowl, and Tanya carefully placed the white rose on top. Rebecca sprinkled the salt, and Maggie poured the blood from the corner of the hamburger tray over all three.

"Are we supposed to say anything?" Maggie asked.

"I don't think so," Tanya said. "I think we just put it in the portal."

The four girls took off their shoes, and Clio picked up the bowl. The group waded slowly into the brook that sprung from the hollow in the tree's base.

"It's *freezing!*" Maggie winced and lifted her pale foot, already mottled purple from the ice-cold water.

Rebecca and Tanya reached into the tree's deep hollow and set the stones in a circle in the shallow water. Clio positioned the bowl in the circle, wedging the rocks into place so it was stable.

"I feel like we should say something," Clio said, "just in case. It seems weird to just put this stuff in the portal and then walk away."

"Let's read the lines from the book again," Tanya suggested. The girls huddled around her, and they read in unison:

"With iron shoe and whitest rose,

Blood and salt,

The door shall close."

"Now what?" Maggie asked. "Is something supposed to happen?"

"I don't think so," Tanya said. "The book doesn't mention some big explosion or anything during the actual sealing."

"Well, that's kind of a letdown," Maggie said.

"Not to me," Rebecca said. "I've had enough drama to last a lifetime! I'm just glad it will finally be over."

"This is just stage one," Tanya said. "Since the portal only opens during the full moon, we won't know for sure it's actually sealed for good until those full moonbeams hit it and it *doesn't* open."

The girls waded out of the stream, and Rebecca

pulled a fluffy white hand towel from her backpack. "Here. Use this." She dried her feet and handed it to Clio.

Clio used the towel and passed it on before slipping into her black ballet flats. "We're definitely coming back during the full moon to make sure the portal can't open anymore, though, right?"

Tanya tucked the book inside a faded canvas backpack covered in badges and pins. "For sure! I need to record the results." She pulled out a pencil and a purple notebook with a peace sign on the cover and opened to a fresh page of graph paper. "It's interesting that it required both iron and salt; I wonder if it causes some kind of chemical reaction. But if so, then what's the catalyst?" She bent over the page, writing a rapid series of notes in tiny, cramped letters.

Maggie finished the knot on her glittery silver sneaker and peered over Tanya's shoulder. "Wait, are you writing up a *lab report*?"

"Mags, you've known Tanya since you were three. How are you literally the only person surprised by this?" Rebecca asked. She pulled a small plastic garbage bag out of the pocket of her jacket and reached for the empty Styrofoam tray on the ground.

"I just still can't believe that anyone would decide to make up homework for themselves! Just . . . *why?*" Maggie grabbed her glittery pink backpack and slung it over one shoulder.

Tanya grinned and tucked the notebook back into her bag. She pulled on a green army surplus jacket. "Don't worry. You'll thank me someday." She slipped her pencil into the breast pocket and straightened the sky-blue wolf pin on the flap.

As the girls left the clearing, Clio turned to scan it one last time, her arched eyebrows knitted with worry.

Rebecca paused next to her. "What's wrong?"

"I don't know," Clio said. "I just got a weird feeling back there."

"Look, we went through some really scary stuff a few weeks ago. We almost lost our lives doing battle with the Night Queen." Rebecca put her arm around Clio. "But it's going to be okay. Now that we've sealed the portal, she won't be able to come into our world again. We're safe."

Tanya joined them. "And hey, in science, at

least, some of the most exciting reactions are things we can't even see. Just because we didn't see anything change right now doesn't mean it didn't work. But don't worry; we'll come back and make certain."

"I know. It's just that I've spent my life watching scary movies with my auntie. And it's never this easy, is all."

"I get it," Rebecca said gently, "but we're not in a movie. Don't worry, Clio. We got this."

Maggie crowded in. "Besides, I wouldn't exactly call everything about this easy. I mean, closing the portal, maybe, but not any of the other stuff. Remember, a few weeks ago Rebecca did almost kill us all and everything."

"Hey, no fair!" Rebecca laughed. "If it had been up to you, we would have been toast!"

Maggie tugged on Rebecca's French braid. "Don't get too high and mighty! I think I managed to save us once or twice, too."

"Oh, don't you two start!" Tanya said, smiling. She pointed to herself. "Because this girl is done with the drama." She pulled the others closer and noticed Clio's face was still clouded with uncertainty. "Come on, I think Clio needs a group hug."

The three girls surrounded Clio and squished in. She squealed and squirmed. "Yay! Okay! Thank you. I feel very loved. You can stop now!"

After one last big squeeze, the girls headed for Kawanna's car. But Clio couldn't help taking one last anxious look back at the clearing behind her.

CHAPTER 2

CLIO HESITATED BEFORE ringing the tarnished brass doorbell of the dilapidated Victorian mansion. No matter how confident she felt as a babysitter, she was always a little nervous meeting a family for the first time. The Lee family had recently moved to Piper, and from the boxes Clio could see, they were still getting settled in the old Plunkett Mansion. The beautiful property had been vacant for years, and Clio was bursting with curiosity to see the inside.

Clio pressed the bell, and a deep gong echoed within the house. Through the front window she saw a tall woman with golden skin and long, straight hair walk briskly to the door, a welcoming smile on her face. Holding her hand was a three-year-old girl in a polka-dot dress and a fuzzy pink cardigan, her straight dark hair pulled into two pigtails.

"Clio!" Mrs. Lee said, opening the door. "We're all so excited to meet you! I'm Sharon, and this is Minna."

Clio crouched down and smiled, holding out her hand to the little girl. "Nice to meet you, Minna." Minna hugged her mother's leg and peeked shyly at Clio from behind Mrs. Lee's hip. After a moment, she put her hand cautiously in Clio's. As they solemnly shook hands, Clio noticed the little girl had pink-and-blue hearing aids in both ears.

"Minna is hard of hearing," Mrs. Lee explained. "It's difficult for her to hear consonants and other soft sounds. The hearing aids help a lot, but she doesn't always catch everything. It can make her a little shy at first.

"Come on in and meet everyone else," Mrs. Lee continued. "Adam's in the back." She called out something in Korean, and Clio heard a man's answering call from the rear of the house. Clio followed Mrs. Lee and Minna down a dark hallway past several dim rooms, each filled with heavy, old-fashioned furniture. "Sorry the house is still such a mess. It came with most of the original furniture, and we're trying to decide what to keep and what to replace. There are some interesting old pieces in here we'd love to preserve if we can."

Clio nodded and smiled. "I love old things, too."

"I have to admit, though, it's a little overwhelming. There are some rooms we haven't even been able to touch yet, so we just closed those doors and decided we'll worry about them later!" She laughed and led Clio through the kitchen and into a walnut-paneled room with a carved marble fireplace.

A broad-shouldered man stood up from the sofa and greeted Clio warmly. His short dark hair was neatly trimmed, and he wore a navy cashmere sweater over a crisp white shirt. Near the fireplace in the corner, an ancient, lanky deerhound stretched and lifted his head drowsily from his bed.

Clio knelt down next to the dog's bed. "What's his name?"

"That's Wesley," Mr. Lee said. "He's eleven. We like to think of him as our first child."

Clio giggled and stroked the dog's shaggy neck. Minna knelt next to her and wrapped her arms around the dog, pressing her face against his bony side. Wesley's tail thumped.

As the Lees gave Clio a tour of the house and explained the family routines, Minna soon warmed up and chattered away excitedly. By the time they reached the little girl's room, she was pulling Clio over to her toy chest to play. Mr. and Mrs. Lee put on their coats and reminded Clio of the list of emergency phone numbers they had left in the kitchen. "The baby monitor is set up down there, too, but I doubt she'll wake up once she goes to bed." Mrs. Lee stroked the top of Minna's head.

"Unless she's having a bath, she keeps her hearing aids in until just before we turn off the light, and then we put them in here." Mr. Lee unscrewed the lid of a small round box on top of the dresser. "And believe me, once this little peanut takes them out, she can sleep through anything!" The parents hugged their daughter goodbye and left.

A few hours later, Minna's toys were put away, her teeth were brushed, and she was snuggled into bed, dressed in a pair of cozy, unicorn-printed pajamas. Her hearing aids were safely tucked away in their container on her dresser. Clio turned on the nightlight, blew Minna a kiss, and headed downstairs to start her homework.

A short time later, Clio stretched and looked at the clock. Her math homework was finished, she had studied for her science quiz, and she had made a pretty good start on her history project. The baby monitor was quiet, and Wesley was snoring by the fireplace. Still thinking about her project, Clio walked into the pantry and pressed the old-fashioned push-button light switch, leaving the door ajar. As she bent down to reach for a granola bar, the light clicked off, plunging her into darkness. She heard the door swing shut behind her.

Startled, Clio stood up quickly, banging her head on a shelf. She heard boxes and cans tumble to the floor. She turned and slid her hand along the wall, searching for the light switch, but she couldn't find it. Instead, her hand closed on the doorknob. Relieved, she turned the knob and pushed on the door.

It didn't move.

She rattled the knob again, but the door stayed

shut. She tried pulling on the knob. Nothing. The door was stuck.

Clio reached into her back pocket for her phone, hoping to use the flashlight to find the light switch. But her pocket was empty, and her cheeks grew hot when she remembered that she had left her phone with her schoolbooks on the kitchen table. *My very first time at the Lees', and they're going to come home to find me accidentally locked in the pantry?*

Clio patted the wall, and at last she found the brass plate of the light switch. She pressed it with a loud click, and the light flickered on. With a sigh, Clio turned to survey the mess she had made of the pantry. Bags of chips and scattered boxes of pasta and crackers littered the floor. A few cans lay on their sides, rolling gently at her feet. She picked up the cans and stacked them neatly back on the shelf. As she bent to gather the boxes, she heard a small click and felt a cool draft against her neck. She looked behind her.

The pantry door had opened by itself.

CHAPTER 3

CLIO GAPED, HER skin prickling. That door had not budged when she'd tried to move it. How had it opened by itself? She reached out one hand and tapped at it. It swung easily on the hinges.

Clio glanced at the fallen boxes of pasta, then back at the empty doorway. She dragged a heavy bag of dog food over to the door, propping it open, and bent over to gather the boxes. The bag rustled slightly behind her, and Clio whipped her head around. Had something moved? The door stayed in place.

She hurried to put the boxes away, keeping one

eye on the pantry doorway. She shoved a granola bar in her pocket and grasped the doorknob firmly before scooting the dog-food bag back into place and stepping out of the pantry. She clicked off the light and closed the door behind her.

Clio's books and papers were exactly where she had left them. Wesley slept soundly in the TV room. Everything was still. Images of supernatural creatures flitted at the edges of her thoughts, but she pushed them away. *There's no way it could happen again*, Clio thought. *This is just an old house. Doors get stuck.* She looked back at the pantry. *And then unstuck . . .*

Clio walked over to the baby monitor. She could hear Minna's even breathing. She checked the back door. Locked and bolted. *Maybe I'll finish my homework next to Wesley*, Clio decided. She stacked the books and slid them across the table toward her chest. As her hand closed around her phone, it let out a sharp *buzz!* and Clio jumped. Her math book slipped out of her arms. She grinned wryly and shook her head at her skittishness. She picked up the phone and saw the text was from Tanya.

how's the new babysitting gig?

Clio smiled and typed back.

<3 the family! house got me
a little freaked tho.

ikr? spooky looking!

no i got locked in the pantry

!!! do u need help???

no the door just got stuck.
im fine now.
just finishing hw.

k. weird. glad ur ok

ttyl

When Clio next checked the time, she saw the Lees were due back soon, and she wanted to make sure the house was in order before they got home. She fluffed the sofa cushions, pushed in the kitchen chairs, and checked that there were no dishes in the sink. As she walked into the hallway, she paused by the pantry door. It was closed and the light was off, just as she had left it, yet Clio couldn't help but quicken her step as she passed. *Am I really going to be scared of a* pantry, *just because the door got stuck?* She made herself turn around and stand in front of the door. "There. See? It's just a regular door," she said out loud.

A sound drew her into the dark front hall. A rhythmic ticking, like a mechanical heartbeat. *Tick. Tock. Tick. Tock.* Clio flicked on the hall light to find a tall, antique grandfather clock, its brass pendulum swinging to and fro behind the glass door of its cabinet. *How did I not hear this before?* Clio wondered. Now that she noticed it, the sound was oppressively loud. She examined the clock's face. The Roman numerals were etched into a tarnished silver faceplate. A moving panel behind the plate depicted a midnight sky scattered with twinkling silver stars. A sliver of moon with a woman's face peered impassively out from behind the left edge of the panel.

Clio looked out the front window, but the sky was cloudy. She pulled her phone out of her pocket and texted Tanya.

> what phase of the moon is it rn?

The phone buzzed a few seconds later. Clio grinned. Tanya probably hadn't even looked it up.

> waxing crescent

> thx!

The moon on the clock matched the moon outside. It didn't just mark the hours; it marked the lunar calendar, too. "Neat," Clio whispered. She had read about old clocks like these, but she had never seen one up close. She could see the winding holes in the faceplate, where the Lees inserted the key to keep the clock working. Old clocks had to be wound regularly or else they would stop. The pendulum moved evenly back and forth, making the steady *ticktock* sound that filled the front hall.

The clock was tall, six feet at least. There was something carved on the dark wood at the top of the clock's cabinet. It looked like an owl. Clio stood on her tiptoes to get a better view. She reached out one arm to the clock's cabinet to help her keep her balance. As her hand touched the wood, the ticking stopped.

Worried that she had somehow broken it, Clio stepped back. The ticking resumed. *Sensitive old thing*, Clio thought. Through the front window she could see the sweep of the headlights of the Lees' car coming down the long drive. She heard the gravel crunch as the car pulled in front of the garage behind the house. Smiling, Clio walked down the hallway to the back of the house to let them in.

As she passed the pantry door, her blood froze.

The door was open.

CHAPTER 4

"WAIT, SO THE door was open when you walked by again?" Maggie asked, her eyes wide. She took a bite of her turkey sandwich, dropping a blob of mayo on her pink-and-gold ROCK STAR sweatshirt.

Clio stirred a pinch of wasabi into her dish of soy sauce and dipped her sushi in the mixture. She raised her voice to be heard above the din of the lunchroom. "And the light was on."

Rebecca dropped her backpack on the floor next to the lunch table and slid her tray next to Maggie. "What'd I miss?"

"Clio's just telling us about spending the

night alone in the creepy old Plunkett Mansion. Spooo-key!"

"That's a bit of an exaggeration." Clio took a bite of her sushi. "I was definitely a little freaked out, but it was mostly fine."

"Well, you did still manage to lock yourself in the pantry," Tanya said, scooping a spoonful of hummus onto a pita slice. "Did you tell the Lees about the wonky door?"

"They said they would check it out and make sure it doesn't get stuck again. I just hope it's not, you know, anything . . . weird." Clio wanted to believe that all the girls' supernatural troubles were finally in the past, but she couldn't help but think of the portal again. What if some other nightmare had slipped through at the last full moon?

Tanya picked up a sugar snap pea. "I'm sure it's not. You know how old houses are." She pulled a Sandman comic out of the pocket of her army surplus jacket and flipped it open.

"Maybe," Clio said. She snapped the lid back on her sushi container and tucked it into its matching red bag, waiting for someone else to say something about the Lees' house, but her friends seemed unconcerned. She shrugged it off and pulled a blue-and-white brochure out of her backpack and laid it on the table. "Are any of you applying for the Student Fellowship this year? The winner gets to go to the Student Leadership Conference in New York!"

"Ooh, New York!" Maggie grabbed the brochure and leafed through it. "Ugh. Never mind." She tossed the brochure on the table. "It's just to visit the boring United Nations. Unless it's Broadway, no thanks!"

Tanya shook her head. "It looks cool, but I'm already busy with my project for the National Science Fair competition."

Rebecca finished her Tater Tots and pulled a Tupperware container out of her backpack. "I was thinking about it, but the independent research project looks like a lot of extra work, and I've already signed up for two new baking classes after school. You should definitely do it, though, Clio." She opened the lid. "Anyone want some mistake brownies? I added too much caramel sauce, so they look a hot mess, but they're really good." She passed the container around, and the girls helped themselves.

"Mmm . . . these are amazing, Rebecca," Clio said, leaning back in her chair. She closed her eyes, relishing the flavor, until someone slammed into her chair, almost knocking her over. "Ow!" She opened her eyes to a forest-green backpack milli-meters from her face. "Watch it!"

Trent Conrad pushed his floppy blond bangs out of his eyes and shoved in closer to the table, his backpack jamming into Clio's chest. "Brownies! Sweet!" He crammed a brownie into his mouth and grinned, his braces smeared with chocolate. "Thanks!" Chewed brownie crumbs flew from his mouth. As he bounded away laughing, his back-pack sent Rebecca's Tupperware lid skittering across the cafeteria floor. Trent didn't even turn around.

Maggie's green eyes followed him. "Rebecca, do you think you could make those brownies for tomorrow, too? Maybe he'll come over here again."

Rebecca stood up to rescue the lid, tugging at her vintage RUN DMC shirt. "Ugh, Mags! Seriously?"

"Trent is the worst," Clio added.

Maggie pulled a mirror out of her backpack and checked her reflection, straightening her hot-pink feather earrings. "No way. He's totally funny, and super cute. I don't know why you guys don't get it." Clio and Rebecca looked at each other over her head, and Rebecca shrugged.

A pale boy with glasses and a blue-dyed streak in his bangs picked up the lid and carried it over to Clio. "Hey, did you drop this?"

"Oh, thank you! That's mine!" Rebecca took the lid and dusted it off on her distressed black skinny jeans. She held out the open container of brownies. "Want one?"

"Sure," he said, carefully selecting a brownie. "Thanks." The boy smiled shyly and walked away.

Clio picked up the Student Fellowship brochure and tucked it in her backpack. "Maybe I'll start working on this when I babysit later this week." She looked around at the others, her face clouded. "That pantry thing was a fluke, right? Are you sure I shouldn't be worried?"

"Fooling around with an old door doesn't sound like anything the Night Queen would bother with," Tanya said. "Trust me, you're fine."

"I don't know about that," Maggie said with a twinkle in her eye. "It sounded to me like the beginning of half of my favorite horror movies. I say watch your back."

Clio swallowed thickly, and Rebecca shot Maggie a dirty look.

"What?!" Maggie said. "I was kidding!"

Rebecca shooed a laughing Maggie away. "Listen, if anyone would know something spooky were going on, it would be me, considering all the stuff that happened when I babysat Kyle. But Minna seems normal, and there's no strange whispers or creepy handprints, right?" Clio shook her head, and Rebecca continued, "It honestly just sounds like an old house to me."

Clio felt herself relax. "Okay, good." She picked up her backpack. "Thanks, guys."

The girls headed to class, and Clio listened as the others chatted excitedly about potential Halloween costumes. *I'm lucky to have such good friends*, Clio thought. It was such a relief to hear them so certain that there was nothing to worry about at the Lees' house. Clio thought again about the pantry door and felt a tiny flutter of anxiety. *I just hope that they're right.*

CHAPTER
5

LATER THAT WEEK, Clio could hear the grandfather clock just striking five when she pressed the bell at the Lees' front door. Minna came running down the hall with Mrs. Lee following close behind. As soon as Mrs. Lee unlocked the front door, Minna rushed forward and grabbed Clio's hand, dragging her inside.

"I've been meaning to ask you about that clock," Clio said. "It's really beautiful. I read about clocks like this, that keep track of the moon and the time, but I've never seen one in person."

"We were lucky. It was here with the house

when we moved in. It's such a unique piece, isn't it?" Mrs. Lee said.

"Definitely," Clio agreed. "Do you know the story behind it?"

"There was no mention of it in any of the estate papers," Mrs. Lee said. "It's almost like it popped out of nowhere!"

Minna pulled at Clio's arm and held up a large plastic dinosaur. "Clio! Look what I got!"

"We went to the natural history museum last Sunday, and now she's all about dinosaurs," Mrs. Lee explained. "She's been dying to show you her new collection of dino figurines."

"It's a suchomimus!" Minna cried, carefully enunciating each syllable of the dinosaur's name: *sook-ee-mime-us*.

"I can't wait to play with it!" Clio said. "First I have to finish talking to your mom for a few minutes, and then I'll come up and play with you." The little girl ran upstairs.

"Adam's at the restaurant tonight, and I'll be at a client dinner until about nine. And we sanded the pantry door, so hopefully you won't get stuck again," Mrs. Lee said with a smile. "There's dinner in the fridge for you and Minna, and emergency numbers are on the bulletin board in the kitchen. Have fun!"

Clio and Minna were soon engaged in a complex pretend play with dinosaur figurines and a few stuffed animals thrown into the mix. Minna's suchomimus had just finished giving a dramatic speech when Clio heard something downstairs. She looked at the clock beside Minna's bed. It was almost six o'clock: dinnertime. "It sounds like Wesley's getting hungry. Do you want to help me get our dinner on the table, or do you want to stay up here and play?" Minna didn't look up from her toys, so Clio tapped her on the shoulder and repeated the question so the little girl could read her lips.

Minna looked intently at Clio's face, then smiled in understanding. "Play, please," she said. She turned back to her toys and picked up the apatosaurus. "My baby! Where is my baby?" she said in a high voice, lifting up the bedspread so the figurine could look under the bed.

A slight chill went up Clio's spine as she stood up and walked into the hallway. There hadn't been a missing baby in the game before. As she reached the bottom of the stairs and passed the clock, it let out an earsplitting *bong . . . !* Clio jumped. The chimes sounded five more times to mark the hour.

More of the moon's face was visible on the clock now, and the fading light from the front window revealed the details on the wood carving. There *was* an owl on the top, and she noticed patterns along the sides of the cabinet, too. It looked almost like leaves intermingled with letters. Clio reached out one finger to lightly trace the design. As soon as her fingertip touched the dark wood, the clock stopped ticking. She pulled her finger away. *Tick. Tock.* The clock started again, just like last time. Clio hurried down the hall, casting a nervous glance behind her. No clock could be *that* sensitive.

Wesley waited for her in the kitchen, standing sentry by his bowl. When he saw Clio, he nudged the bowl with his nose, banging it against the raised plastic stand. "Okay, I get the message!" Clio laughed. She petted him and scooped a cup of kibble into his bowl. Tail wagging, he dived into his dish and crunched away.

Clio pulled the two covered plates out of the refrigerator and put the first one in the microwave.

Her thoughts turned back to the clock as she put down two place mats and set the table, laying the cutlery and napkins neatly at each setting. *Why does it stop whenever someone touches it?* She turned the question over and over in her mind as she put the water glasses on the table and walked back to the microwave to heat the second plate.

Wait. Something wasn't right. Clio turned and checked the table again. The knives, forks, and spoons were all missing from the place mats. So were the napkins. Had she only *thought* she set them out? The kitchen was empty. Wesley had finished his meal and lay curled up on the TV-room sofa. *I could have sworn I set the table.* She stared at the bare table and felt a cool breeze flutter through the room, even though the windows were closed. A chill traced its way up the back of her neck. She shook her head. *Nope. Not gonna go there.* She hurriedly reset the table with new silverware and napkins before going upstairs to get Minna.

A few minutes later, they entered the kitchen, and Minna slid into her seat at the table. Clio placed a warm plate in front of her, and the little girl giggled. "You're silly!"

"What do you mean?" Clio asked, sliding her own plate onto the table.

"You gave me two forks!" Minna pointed to the forks sitting side by side at her place. "And two knives! And two spoons!" Clio looked down at her own place setting, shocked to see two sets of cutlery. Her stomach dropped. *I checked that table before I went upstairs. I know I did.*

"How did you make this?" Minna asked. She opened her paper napkin and held it up. It was cut into a chain of little girls holding hands. "Will you teach me?"

Clio unfolded her own napkin. A string of little girls stretched across her lap. "I didn't make this. I guess your mom must have made them as a surprise for you."

Minna shook her head. "My mom doesn't do art."

"Oh." Clio smoothed the napkin in her lap. "I guess she must have bought them, then." She stood up. "You go ahead and eat before your dinner gets cold. I'll put these away." Her hands shook as she gathered the extra silverware, and a fork clattered under the table. Clio bent to pick it up.

The floor below the table was scattered with snips of paper napkin.

· · · · ·

Clio barely touched her food, and when dinner was finished, she settled Minna in front of a movie in the TV room. The little girl nestled against Wesley and pulled the blanket over both of them. "I'll come watch with you as soon as I finish cleaning up our dinner," Clio said.

Back in the kitchen, she pulled out her phone and called Tanya.

"What's up?" Tanya asked.

"I'm freaking out, and I kind of need you to lay some science on me, because otherwise I might lose it over here," Clio said. She told Tanya what had happened with the cutlery and napkins. "So what's going on? There has to be a logical explanation, right? One that isn't supernatural? Please say yes."

"Sure. Yes."

"Okay. What is it?"

Tanya paused. "Well, maybe when you unfolded the napkins, all the snipped parts fell out onto the floor, and you just didn't notice them."

Clio cleared the plates from the table. "I feel like we probably would have seen them drop, but maybe, I guess. . . . But what about the silverware?"

"Maybe you just got distracted and didn't notice that you had already set the table, and you set it twice. Could the silverware have been, like, camouflaged against the place mat or something?"

Clio rinsed the plates and put them in the dishwasher. "Um, no. I would have seen them. I'm telling you I set the table, they were gone, I set the table again, and then they were back. How would that happen? What's the logical explanation for that?"

Tanya paused. "I know there's a logical explanation, but that doesn't necessarily mean we know what it is," she said slowly.

"Seriously?! How is that helpful?" Clio swept the scattered napkin bits into a dustpan.

"Hey, I'm doing my best! I'm not even there to see it! Can you take pictures and send them?"

Clio looked at the napkin snips in the trash can. "It's too late now. I cleaned everything up."

"Well, if it happens again, send photos, okay? In the meantime, just try to relax and have fun."

"Tanya"—Clio lowered her voice slightly—"what if it's the Night Queen? What if she's back?"

"The portal only opens during the full moon, and we sealed that thing; don't worry." Tanya sighed. "And besides, do you really think the Night Queen would bother cutting paper dolls? I'm sure everything's fine. Call me later."

Clio shoved the phone back in her pocket and joined Minna in the TV room. Soon the movie had her laughing, and when the credits rolled, Clio looked down to see Minna curled up against her, eyelids heavy. "Come on, Minna Mouse," Clio whispered, helping the drowsy girl off the couch and half carrying her up the stairs.

Soon Minna was tucked snugly in bed. Clio slipped out of the room with a smile, but the warm, cozy feeling dissipated as she headed back down the stairs. The ticking of the clock rattled her nerves, and something rustled behind the pantry door as she passed by. "It's nothing," she whispered to herself, gritting her teeth. "It's just an old house."

Besides, even if it's more than that, what am I gonna do? Clio thought. *Grab Minna and run out of* the house screaming? *Tell her parents they have to move?* No way. If there was something supernatural behind what had happened in the kitchen tonight, Clio was pretty sure she didn't want to know. It was a few forks and some napkin pieces. Maybe if she didn't think about it too much, she could just forget it ever happened.

Careful not to look too closely around the room, Clio switched the TV to a music channel and slid her laptop out of her backpack. She pulled up the fellowship application website and logged in.

She never once noticed the shriveled, misshapen face that watched her through the window.

CHAPTER
6

THE CREATURE FEATURES costume shop was one of Clio's favorite places in the world. Her aunt had rented the storefront on Coffin Street, with its tiny apartment in back, just over a month ago. Tucked between a dusty antique store and an empty vacuum-repair shop, the crumbling facade was utterly unlike the vibrant, welcoming space they had created inside.

Rich fabrics and wild costumes hung side by side with feather boas and vintage evening gowns. The glass counter sported sparkling costume jewelry interspersed with plastic vampire fangs and fake blood capsules. Shelves of hats, wigs, and masks lined one wall, and the carved wooden bookcases along the back were stuffed with old curios and leather-bound books. Clio spent almost every day there after school.

The bell tinkled above the door. "We have a customer, Aunt Kawanna!" Clio looked up from the homework she had spread across the counter and waved to the pale boy who slouched in carrying a bent manila folder with wrinkled papers sticking out of it. His shaggy dark hair had a bright blue streak in the front that almost matched the blue eyes behind his dark-framed glasses. He wore an unzipped gray hoodie over a faded navy Rocket Cats concert T-shirt. She recognized him from the cafeteria, but she didn't know his name.

Kawanna sauntered through the doorway from her office at the back of the store. Gold bangles jingled merrily on her coppery brown wrist as she patted the bun of tightly coiled dreadlocks on the top of her head. "May I help you?"

The boy laid his folder on the counter. "I'm not sure. I hope so, though."

Kawanna gestured to the racks of brightly colored clothes and the shelves. "Well, even if we don't have exactly what you need, I'm sure we can put together something that might work." She pointed to the Godzilla-print A-line skirt she was wearing. "And if you don't need it today, I can also do custom designs."

The boy smiled. "My name's Ethan. Ethan Underwood." He turned to Clio. "I think I've seen you around school."

Clio introduced herself and her aunt. "So what can we do for you?"

Ethan opened the folder. "Well, my great-grandma Moina used to have a business here in town, and we were thinking about opening it up again."

"A family business," Clio said. "Cool. What's your great-grandma going to do?"

"Oh, she died before I was born."

"Oh."

"It's just going to be me running the business."

"Uh-huh." Clio drifted back over to her home-work. This kid was a little strange.

"I was wondering if you might let me put up a flyer in your window. It would really help get the word out." He slid a few wrinkled papers aside and pulled out a small, smooth poster with elaborate artwork.

Curious, Clio put down her pencil and craned her neck across the counter. "Is that a picture of a ghost walking a dog?"

Ethan blushed. "Why? Is that too weird?"

Clio pulled the poster closer. "Well, it is weird, but it's really good. Did you draw it?"

Ethan's cheeks grew pinker. "Yeah."

Kawanna held up the poster. "You have quite a talent, Ethan. The artwork is beautiful. Does this say *Snout of This World* at the top?"

"That's the name of my business. I'm kind of a one-stop shop. I've been doing dog walking and petsitting for my neighbors for a few years, and I also do animal communication."

Clio and her aunt looked at Ethan blankly. "I'm a pet psychic," he explained. "I'm pretty good at it. The other day I was eating breakfast, and I could sense that my dog really wanted a bite. It was like a total mind meld!"

Clio picked up her pencil and turned back to her homework. "Doesn't every dog want a bite of your breakfast? Isn't that kind of what dogs do?"

"I don't think so. This was different. It's like I could see a little speech bubble over her head: *Sausage . . . I want . . . sausage!* So I gave it to her, and guess what, she loved it!"

"Okay, well, good luck with that," Clio said, opening her history book. She started to read a sentence, then closed the book again. "Wait a minute. You have a ghost in your drawing. What does that have to do with dog walking?"

Ethan slapped his hand to his forehead. "Oh, right! That's my newest line of services. I have Great-Grandma Moina to thank for that."

"The dead one," Clio offered, raising one eyebrow.

"Be nice!" Kawanna hissed, kicking her under the counter. She carried the poster over to a colorful bulletin board near the front of the store and tacked it to one corner.

Ethan opened his folder and took out a tattered black-and-white photograph of a young woman. She was seated in a high-backed, ornately carved chair behind a cloth-covered table with three lit candles in the middle. A book, a bell, and a wooden mallet were arranged neatly on the table in front of her. The woman wore a long string of pearls over a velvet dress, and a black lace veil draped over her hair. Her heavy, dark eyebrows were stark against her pale skin, and her light eyes were rimmed with kohl. She looked like an actress in a silent movie. On the back of the photo a date was written in old-fashioned cursive: October 29, 1928.

"Was that your great-grandmother?" Clio asked.

"Yeah," Ethan said. "Well, technically I think she's my great-great-grandmother; I kind of lose track of the greats. Anyway, she was pretty famous back in her day. She traveled all over the world as a spiritualist."

Clio pulled the photo closer. "What's a spiritualist? Is that like a religious thing?"

"No, she held séances. She was a medium."

Kawanna laid the photo down and turned to the bookshelves behind the counter. She pulled out an old book with an orange linen cover and opened it up. "Spiritualism was all the rage back in the 1920s. Folks would hold séances and use Ouija boards, all in the hopes of communicating with the dead."

Clio dropped her pencil. "Wait, so your great-great-grandmother used to talk to ghosts?"

Ethan nodded. "And I think I've inherited her power."

Clio stared at Ethan, her mind reeling with questions. But before she could ask any, a rowdy group of college students burst through the door, all talking and laughing. "We have an epic party to plan, and we need costumes!" one of them shouted. They swarmed across the shop, pawing everything in sight.

Clio and Kawanna hurried over. "Sorry, Ethan. I'll be back in a minute," Clio called behind her.

A tall, tan guy with a mane of shaggy blond hair tapped Clio on the shoulder. "Hey, do you have any scary werewolf costumes?" he asked.

Clio grabbed something from a rack and handed it to him. "Changing rooms are in the back." She pointed down the hall to two brightly painted doors just past Kawanna's locked office.

She glanced back to the counter where she had left Ethan, but he was gone. Clio heard the jingle of the bell and caught a glimpse of a gray hoodie slipping out the front door. She stared thoughtfully after him for a moment.

Was Ethan serious? Could he really talk to ghosts?

CHAPTER
7

THE SUN WAS just beginning to set behind the trees as the four girls walked along the path toward the clearing in the woods. It was the night of the full moon. Maggie and Rebecca chatted quietly up ahead, Rebecca's sleek ponytail bouncing along as she walked. Tanya followed behind them, taking copious notes in her lab book. "On our way to test portal and make sure seal is secure," she mumbled to herself, her pencil scratching across the page. She glanced around her. "No sign of change in general environment." She consulted a thermometer on the key chain attached to the zipper of her army surplus jacket. "Temperature: twelve-point-eight degrees Celsius." She logged the number into a neatly drawn table at the top of one page.

Clio brought up the rear, her hands shoved into the pockets of her navy peacoat. Her eyes darted to follow every rustle in the undergrowth. "Guys, do you hear something?"

Rebecca and Maggie stopped their conversation. "Sorry, what was that, Clio?" Rebecca asked.

"Shh!" Clio held up her hand. "I think something might be following us." The woods were still. The girls waited.

"I don't hear anything," Maggie said.

"Well, obviously not right this second. It must have stopped because it heard us listening."

"*What* stopped?" Maggie asked irritably.

Clio peered into the darkening brush. "I don't know. Whatever's following us."

Tanya pulled her nose out of her lab book. "Wait, there's something following us?"

"I don't know," Clio said. "That's what I'm trying to figure out."

"Maybe we should spread out and search for it," Rebecca suggested.

"Are you kidding?" Maggie asked. "Have you

paid attention to any scary movie we've ever watched? Spreading out is like the kiss of death! If something's following us, we need to stick together so it can't pick us off one by one." She grabbed Rebecca's hand.

"What's going to pick us off one by one?" Tanya asked, looking around.

"I don't know!" Clio shouted, exasperated. "I just heard noises in the woods, like something might be following us!"

"Oh," Tanya said. "Then it's probably just a squirrel."

Clio frowned. "It sounded bigger than a squirrel."

"How big?" Maggie asked. She huddled closer to Rebecca.

"I don't know. Bigger. I heard rustling noises. Branches moving. Stuff like that."

"Maybe your aunt Kawanna got tired of waiting for us in the car and decided to come help," Rebecca said.

Clio checked her phone. "She would call or text first, and I haven't heard from her. Besides, I don't think she could even find the clearing, anyway. Just like anything else supernatural in this town, it's basically invisible to adults."

"Well, I still don't hear anything," Rebecca said, "so let's just get to the clearing. The full moon's going to rise soon, and we want to make sure the portal to the Nightmare Realm is closed once and for all so the Night Queen can't get through again."

"Good idea," Tanya said. "If we miss it, we'll have to wait almost another month to check again."

The girls huddled closer together, arriving at the clearing as the last red rays of sunlight dipped behind the tree line. They pulled out their flashlights. Tanya reached into her backpack and removed a few camping lanterns, which she set up around the clearing.

"What'll we do if the portal doesn't close?" Clio asked.

Tanya shrugged. "Experiments fail all the time." She strapped a headlamp over her short hair and switched it on. "Then we'll just have to go back to the drawing board, I guess."

"That's comforting." Maggie shivered and zipped up her pink fleece jacket.

Rebecca patted Maggie on the back. "Don't worry; we did a lot of research to figure this out. It's gonna work," she said confidently. She shined her flashlight into the open base of the tree. "Look, see? The bowl's still in there, right where we left it."

Clio hovered behind Rebecca's shoulder and peered into the dark hollow. "The portal only opens during the full moon, right? So say we did the ceremony wrong and didn't actually seal it forever. Has anyone thought about the possibility that if we messed up and it does still open tonight, then something might come *out* of it?"

"Well, not until just now, I hadn't!" Maggie looked nervously at the tree's trunk and picked up a stick and waved it menacingly, taking a few experimental swipes in the air.

"Good idea," Clio said. She and Rebecca found the biggest sticks they could and held them at the ready. Maggie nudged Tanya.

"Don't look at me," Tanya said. "I'm not fighting anything." She held up two fingers in a peace sign.

"Useless," Maggie sighed, throwing an arm around Tanya. Tanya grinned and rested her head on Maggie's shoulder.

The heavens deepened to a rich blue, and a few stars began to twinkle. "Look, there's Jupiter," Tanya said, pointing to a bright point of light near the horizon.

Soon the full moon rose into the velvet night sky, and Clio could feel the tension build in the clearing around them, like the forest itself was holding its breath.

Clio jumped when she heard a crash in the brush behind her. She turned and rushed toward the sound. "Who's there?"

"Clio! We need to stay together!" Maggie cried.

Clio saw a hunched, monkeylike shape dart in the shadows beyond the clearing. "There's something out there!" Heart pounding, she pushed aside the thick branches and pressed deeper into the trees. The figure hopped away, just at the edge of her vision. Clio left the light of the clearing and stepped into the darkness of the forest beyond.

Suddenly, something grabbed her arm and yanked her backward. Clio screamed.

"Relax! It's just me!" Maggie said, dropping Clio's arm. "Where were you going?"

"I saw something in the woods. It wasn't an animal, and it wasn't a person. It felt . . . wrong."

Maggie dragged Clio back toward the lanterns. "So you were just going to follow it by yourself in the dark? Great idea." She picked a twig from Clio's twist-out.

"But what if it's connected to the portal?" Clio asked, straining to see where the creature had gone.

Tanya called out to them, her voice thick with tension. "Guys, you better come back. I think something's about to happen!"

Maggie and Clio hurried back to find Rebecca and Tanya standing at the edge of the brook. Rebecca's flashlight beam shone steadily on the bowl inside the tree's hollow, and Tanya snapped photos with the digital camera that hung from a strap around her neck. She dropped the camera, checked her thermometer, and grabbed her notebook. "Temperature is dropping steadily. Current read: seven-point-two degrees Celsius and falling rapidly . . . four-point-eight and still falling . . . two-point-three . . . zero and still falling . . ."

Clio rubbed one arm with her free hand, trying to stay warm. Her breath came out in clouds. Her teeth chattered. She felt Maggie grab her arm, her fingers squeezing her tightly.

She heard a cracking sound and looked down to see a thin layer of ice forming over the brook. Before her eyes, the ice turned white and thickened until the brook was frozen through.

With an earsplitting crack the ice shattered, cleaving the bowl in two. An unearthly howl echoed through the darkness, and then all sound stopped. There was a hiss of steam, and a feathery plume of smoke curled up from the bowl and disappeared into the sky.

Clio stopped shivering, and her grip loosened on her flashlight. The brook burbled along, with no sign of the ice that had covered it moments before. The night sounds of the forest began again. Tanya checked her thermometer. "Ten-point-six degrees Celsius and rising," she noted.

Maggie dropped her hand from Clio's arm. "So is it sealed forever? Did we do it?"

Rebecca swept the flashlight beam deeper into the tree's hollow. "Jeez, I hope so! That would be an awful lot of drama if it hadn't."

Tanya slipped out of her black Vans and peeled

off her socks. "Well, there's only one way to find out." She stepped into the frigid water and gasped. "Still really cold!" The other girls stripped off their shoes and socks and picked their way into the brook.

They crowded into the tree's hollow. Rebecca's flashlight illuminated the jagged crack that divided the bowl into two halves, the salt and blood now a dried red crust that rimmed the edges. "Whoa," Maggie whispered. She pointed to the horseshoe. It had also cracked in half. "I don't know what it was, but *something* definitely happened."

Tanya bent over her notebook, making a quick sketch. "If the portal hasn't sealed, we should be able to walk through it like the last full moon." She slipped around the bowl and reached for the far wall of the tree. "It's solid," she said. "I'm touching the inside of the tree. Here, come check."

The other girls squeezed around the bowl and pushed against the back wall of the hollow. "It's definitely closed for good," Rebecca said. Clio shut her eyes and breathed a sigh of relief.

Maggie brushed her hands together. "Looks like our work here is done!" She ducked out of the tree's opening and splashed her way to the brook's edge. "Back to Creature Features for some hot cocoa and a good scary movie?"

Rebecca moaned. "Not another scary movie. You know I can't stand them!"

"Oh, you love it!" Maggie said, tying her rainbow shoelaces in a quick double knot.

Clio helped Tanya pack up the remaining gear while Rebecca scanned the rest of the clearing. "Looks like we've got everything."

"Not everything," Maggie said. "We forgot the bowl!" She moved toward the hollow to retrieve it, but Clio grabbed her arm.

"Let's leave the bowl in there."

Maggie turned to look at Clio, a questioning look on her face. "Why?"

Clio's eyes scoured the darkness beyond the clearing.

"Just in case."

CHAPTER 8

BACK AT THE costume shop, Kawanna scanned the bookshelves behind the counter, her orange-and-black-striped nails running along the spines of the vast array of DVD cases. "How about *House on Haunted Hill*? It's a classic, and part of it was filmed at an old mansion not too far from where I used to live in LA."

"Were you in this one, too, Kawanna?" Maggie asked. Clio's aunt used to work as an actress in Hollywood. Her days doing bit parts in B horror movies began a lifelong collection of monster-movie memorabilia and a deep love for anything scary.

"How old do you think I am, Maggie?" Kawanna

clutched at her heart in mock dismay. "This was way before my time, thank you very much!" Maggie laughed, and Kawanna waved the DVD case above her head. "Now, if everyone's finally ready"—her eyes grew wide—"let the terror begin!" The girls hooted and pumped their fists, but Rebecca's cheer was tepid. Noticing the nervous expression on Rebecca's face, Kawanna gave her a reassuring pat. "Don't worry, Rebecca. It's an old movie, and the special effects aren't particularly good. I doubt you'll find it very scary." Rebecca smiled gratefully.

Maggie scoffed. "Becks, a few weeks ago we faced down *real* monsters, and you're still afraid of an old horror movie? It's not even in color!"

"I'm not afraid. I just don't like the jump-scares. And the gory parts."

"You've just described pretty much everything that makes a good horror movie."

"I know!" Rebecca said. "That's why I don't like them."

"And that's exactly why I do!" Maggie replied.

"To each their own," Kawanna said, and winked at Rebecca.

Clio, dressed in a vintage I ♥ NY T-shirt and Eiffel Tower–print pajama bottoms, took the DVD case from her aunt and skimmed the summary on the back. "Oh, I remember this one. I was terrified of that dancing skeleton when I was little!"

"Hey!" Maggie cried. "No spoilers!"

Clio grinned as she popped the DVD into the player and turned on the TV that Kawanna had mounted to the wall in one corner of the shop. "No spoilers, huh? Well, then I guess I won't tell you about the part where—"

"Noooo!" Maggie shrieked. She covered her ears. "La la la la la!"

"Oh, don't tease her, Clio," Kawanna chided gently. She swept her blue-and-red-print silk robe behind her and stepped into her fuzzy green monster slippers before walking down the back hallway to her office.

"*You're* telling *me* not to tease? That's a good one, Auntie!" Clio called after her. She joined Maggie and Rebecca in setting up an array of beanbag chairs, sleeping bags, and air mattresses for the sleepover in the store. Kawanna returned to the front of the shop, her arms full of blue-and-gold-brocade throw pillows. Maggie looked up to thank her and saw a leering werewolf standing over her instead. She screamed.

Kawanna laughed and pulled off the snarling rubber mask she had slipped on. "Sorry, Maggie. But you did say you love jump-scares!"

"Gee, Maggie, we faced down *real* monsters, so what are you so *afraid* of?" Rebecca said, laughing.

Maggie blushed and playfully shoved her friend's shoulder as Rebecca high-fived Kawanna.

Clio shook her head with a wry grin. "Seriously, Auntie. I wonder why I ever allow you around any of my friends." From pretending to be a zombie to putting fake worms in the girls' snacks, Clio's aunt's pranks were legendary.

Tanya, dressed in a faded black Doctor Who T-shirt and flannel pajama pants patterned with flying saucers, carried a huge bowl of buttery popcorn in from the kitchen of Kawanna's little apartment behind the store. She set it down in the middle of the floor, and the other girls eagerly dived in.

"Hey," Tanya said. "Save some for the movie." She glanced up at the movie's menu screen on the TV. "Ugh, ghosts. Do you guys really believe in them?"

Maggie grabbed another handful of popcorn, dripping butter onto her leopard-print pajamas. "Um, hello? Were we not just at the same supernatural portal?"

"The Night Queen is one thing, but ghosts are something different," Tanya said. "Scientifically speaking, creatures certainly exist in other worlds, with connecting portals. Quantum physics calls it the multiverse. But ghosts? Spirits of people who died, hanging around and haunting things? I mean, why would they do that?"

"Oh, I don't know," Clio said. "That doesn't seem so weird to me." Thoughts of the Lees' house flickered through her mind. Could it be a ghost that had locked her in the pantry and messed up the kitchen table? She pushed the thought away. *Nobody locked me in the pantry; I just got stuck. And I was distracted when I set the table.*

Rebecca shrugged out of her blue-gray cashmere robe and pushed up the sleeves of her cupcake-print pajama top. "My Nai Nai always said we should treat ghosts as a fact of life. They're just *there*. You don't bother them, and they don't bother you, like a spider in the corner of the bathroom."

"Um. No," Maggie said. "If there's a spider in my bathroom, that sucker's going down."

"Murderer," Tanya muttered, with a smile on her face.

Maggie grinned back and pointed to herself. "Me? A spider murderer?" She nodded. "Yeah, I can definitely live with that label."

"But what about ghosts?" Rebecca asked.

"Are you asking if I would kill a ghost?" Maggie said.

"Not kill it," Rebecca said. "But say there was a ghost in your house. Would you be scared, would you try to make friends with it, or would you just ignore it and hope it goes away?"

Maggie thought for a moment. "I bet I'd be scared at first, but I don't know . . . if it didn't do anything too weird, I'd probably make friends with it if I could. Or at least try to find out what it wanted."

Clio untacked the Snout of This World flyer from the bulletin board on the wall and carried it over to the group. "There's a kid at school who says he talks to them."

Maggie snatched the flyer. "No way! Who?" She shoved the popcorn bowl aside and bent over the mini-poster. Tanya and Rebecca crowded in to see.

"Remember that quiet kid from the cafeteria? The one with the blue streak in his hair? His great-great-grandmother was a medium. She held séances and stuff." Clio quickly filled them in on everything Ethan had told her and Kawanna.

"I remember him. He's kind of cute!" Maggie looked more closely at Ethan's artwork. "I can't decide if that's really cool or really creepy."

Tanya idly scanned the flyer. "Most of those old mediums were proven frauds. Once when I visited my grandparents in LA, they took me to a fake séance at the Magic Castle, this cool magicians' club, and we got to see all the tricks they used to make people think there were ghosts in the room. It was fun."

"Don't tell that to Ethan. He's pretty sure he inherited her powers."

"But did he?" Maggie asked. "I mean, did you see him do it?"

"What, like we were gonna ask him to do a

demonstration?" Clio asked. She tacked the flyer back to the bulletin board.

Maggie sighed. "I guess not, but do you think he really can?"

Clio shrugged. "I don't know. What do you think, Auntie?"

Kawanna laid a silver tray on the counter and scooped tiny marshmallows into mugs of cocoa. "Well, I've been in enough scary movies to know how easy it is to fake a ghost; Tanya's certainly right about that. But I've heard plenty of stories over the years from good friends who think they've seen one. It's enough to make me wonder, anyway." She passed colorful mugs of cocoa around to the girls and picked up the last one, which was shaped like the head of Frankenstein's monster.

"Maybe you could invite Ethan to do a séance in the shop," Maggie suggested. She looked around the room. "I bet a lot of kids at school would be pretty into it. It could bring in some new business."

Rebecca folded her arms. "Come on, Mags. We just finished solving one supernatural problem. Do we really need to go looking for more?"

"Good point," Maggie said, remembering their

last adventure. She shivered. "Maybe we should just enjoy the land of the living for a while."

"Don't get too excited about the land of the living just yet," Kawanna said, "because we're about to meet a whole bunch of ghosts!" She flicked off the lights and started the movie.

The picture went black, and a woman's scream reverberated through the speakers. Kawanna squeezed in with the girls, and they huddled around the popcorn as the spooky opening scene filled the screen.

CHAPTER 9

CLIO TUCKED MINNA into bed with her favorite dinosaur toy and gave her a final good-night hug. The little girl's hearing aids were already put away, so Clio leaned down to speak carefully and clearly into Minna's ear. "I had so much fun with you tonight!"

"Me, too." Minna smiled sleepily and snuggled deeper into the covers. Clio switched off the light and walked toward the stairs, half wishing she had some excuse to keep Minna up past her bedtime. Minna's sunny personality made it easy for Clio to relax and forget her fears about the old mansion, but as soon as she tucked the little girl in,

Clio felt her senses heighten. Every tiny creak of the hallway floor felt as loud as a firecracker, and she had to will herself not to look behind her.

Clio passed the closed doors along the hallway and took in the dark green wallpaper patterned with twisting black vines. She loved antiques and old buildings, but the Plunkett Mansion felt oppressive, as though a dark cloud hung over the house, soaking into its walls.

Only Minna's room felt like a bright ray of sunshine, with its pastel blue paint and cheerful elephant-patterned curtains. What a relief it would be when the whole house was finished and the rest of the rooms were just as inviting.

Back downstairs, Clio washed the dishes and looked out into the backyard. It had always been too late in the day to play with Minna outside, but she knew that the property stretched back for several acres. At the bottom of the sloping lawn, she could see the moon reflecting on a small pond and the pale outline of a crumbling stone pavilion. If she came to babysit during the day, it might be fun to take Minna down to the pond for a picnic. It would be good to spend time outside and enjoy some fresh air and sunshine, away from the house's shadow. Just imagining it made Clio feel more relaxed, and she made a mental note to ask Mrs. Lee about it.

Clio had just dried her hands when Wesley trotted over, a ratty old tennis ball in his mouth. "Do you want to play fetch?" she asked. His tail wagged, and he dropped the ball at her feet. She tossed it in the air, and he jumped up and caught it. "Good boy!" Clio cheered.

He dropped it at her feet again. This time she tossed it farther, and it sailed out of the kitchen and into the dark dining room. Wesley scampered off to chase it, but he stopped at the edge of the dining room doorway. He stiffened, hackles rising, his tail now a rigid straight line. He backed away from the room, a low growl in his throat.

He shook himself and sneezed before slinking over to Clio and leaning against her legs. He was panting, his chest heaving. "What's wrong, sweet boy?" She crouched down and put an arm around him, and he curled into her, whining.

She stood up. "Let's go see what spooked you." Even when Clio had been scared herself, Wesley had always remained unperturbed. She found herself holding her breath as she walked to the dining room doorway and flicked on the dim overhead light. She was relieved to find nothing amiss. "See? There's nothing for either of us to be scared of." She turned back to the dog, but he had retreated to his bed in the TV room.

Clio looked around the empty dining room. What could have scared the dog so much? A massive dining table dominated the room, its curving legs carved to look like lions. The elaborate, high-backed dining chairs were upholstered with threadbare red velvet. A large mirror with a gilded frame hung above a dark wood credenza, opposite a wall covered with framed black-and-white photos of people in old-fashioned clothing standing in front of a house. Crimson wallpaper flocked with black velvet stretched to meet heavy crown molding, and the dusty crystal chandelier made the ceiling seem like it was closing in on her. *I don't blame him. It is a little creepy in here*, Clio thought. Clio moved closer to the old photos, her attention caught by one particular picture. In it, a white family stared stone-faced at the camera. The mother had a tiny corseted waist, and she wore a dark dress with a long skirt and puffy sleeves, her blond hair coiled beneath a wide-brimmed hat trimmed with feathers. She held a bundled-up baby in her arms. The dark-haired father was dressed in a long-coated suit over a white shirt with a high collar. His tall black top hat was angled slightly forward on his head, as though pointing to his bristly mustache, and he carried a cane. In front of them, two little girls in white dresses held hands. Their fair hair was cut in straight bangs, and each had a white bow at the top of her head. Their pale eyes were barely visible against their milk-white faces.

Clio looked more closely at the house in the background, and she immediately recognized the turret and the wraparound porch. "Cool," she whispered. "This must be the family who built this house." She carefully lifted the picture from the wall and turned it over to look for a date on the back. Scrawled near the frame were the words *T. D. Plunkett and family, 1892.*

A cool breath of air curled against the back of her neck. Behind her, the crystals in the chandelier began to rattle violently against one another. Her shadow shrank and grew on the wall in front of her with the wildly swinging light. She gasped and spun around. The room was empty and still, but the chandelier continued to sway, the crystal droplets tinkling against one another like ice in a glass.

Goose bumps rose on Clio's skin, and a cold feeling of dread crept over her.

She slowly hung the picture back on the wall, scanning the room as she did so. Nothing moved.

Wesley's ball lay at the edge of the carpet, and she knelt down to retrieve it. Just as her fingers brushed the ball, it rolled out of her reach. She leaned forward and reached for it again. The ball rolled farther away, an inch or two out of her grasp. Fighting rising panic, Clio crawled forward and extended her hand.

The ball rolled away from her hand and disappeared under the table.

Clio's breath caught in her throat. *Just leave it. Just leave the ball and get out of this room*, she thought.

But another part of her rankled at the thought of being spooked so easily. *It's just a ball. It's not like it can do anything.* She crouched on the floor, paralyzed by indecision.

Finally, heart pounding, Clio slithered between

the dining chairs into the shadows beneath the table. The second her hand closed around the ball, she hopped to her feet. "I'm okay!" she said breathlessly to no one. The room waited, silent and expectant. She could *feel* something watching her.

"I'm okay," she whispered to herself again. The words rung hollow.

Clio ran out of the room, shutting off the light behind her. She dropped the old tennis ball into the trash can under the sink and firmly closed the cabinet door.

She took a moment to check the baby monitor before grabbing her backpack and retreating to the TV room. Wesley was still in his bed, and he barely stirred when Clio clicked the remote and searched for the goofiest sitcom she could find, anything to get her mind off what had happened in the dining room. Her heart was still pounding.

The house was calm and quiet again; the only sound was the ticking of the hall clock. Clio felt herself begin to relax as the final credits eventually rolled across the screen. She checked the monitor in the kitchen, comforted by the sound of Minna's slow, even breathing. She poured herself a glass of ice water. The clinking ice made her think of the chandelier, and she shuddered. She poured the ice water into Wesley's bowl instead.

Clio checked her phone. The Lees would be home in less than an hour. She pulled a novel out of her backpack. She could probably finish a few more chapters before they arrived.

Clio had just turned to a fresh chapter when she heard the stairs creak. Then, a slow, deliberate bouncing: *thud . . . thud . . . thud . . .*

Something was moving down the stairs.

Clio stood up, her skin crawling. She knew what the sound was.

Stomach sinking, she walked into the front hallway.

There, at the bottom of the stairs, was Wesley's tennis ball.

Clio stared at the ball in horror. She had thrown it in the trash earlier that night. She recognized the shredded spot where the rubber shone through.

Afraid to breathe, she slowly bent down to pick it up, half expecting it to roll away from her fingers. Just as her fingertips grazed the worn yellow fuzz, a

metallic gong tore the air. She screamed and jumped back.

It was the hall clock. Clio gritted her teeth.

The chimes continued, loud and relentless, boring into her head, as Clio rushed to the kitchen.

A part of her hoped that she would be wrong, that this was a different ball that had somehow tumbled down the stairs. Accidentally. And very, very slowly. Her mind tried to grasp the idea and hold on to it, but she knew how foolish it sounded.

She hurriedly opened the cabinet under the sink and peered into the empty trash can. She looked back to where Wesley was still sleeping in the TV room. He hadn't moved. There was no point in asking herself how the ball had gotten from inside the trash can to the top of the stairs and back down again. Despite what Tanya might say, there was no logical way to explain it.

Clio dropped the ball back in the garbage and slammed the cupboard shut. She leaned against the counter and looked across the empty rooms. As much as she wanted to, she couldn't deny it any longer.

There was something supernatural inside the house.

CHAPTER
10

CLIO SENT A text to her aunt and friends:

> BIG PROBLEM. MEET AT CF
> 9AM TOMORROW.

By the time the Lees returned home, Clio was waiting, her backpack neatly tucked by the door. After chatting with both parents for a few moments, Clio climbed into the passenger seat of Mrs. Lee's SUV. She was bursting with questions. She didn't want to scare the Lees, but she needed to find out if they had seen anything strange, too.

"I had fun playing fetch with Wesley tonight," Clio said. "When he dropped his ball in the dining room, I noticed some neat old pictures on the walls. I guess the house must have a really cool history, huh?"

Mrs. Lee smiled. "Apparently, the property belonged to the original family for a couple generations. The last Plunkett to inhabit the house was a distant cousin, Henry Plunkett. He was a bachelor who lived alone. When he passed away, the house was inherited by another distant relative who lived across the country, so it sat vacant for ten years until we bought it."

Clio chose her words carefully. "It must have been a funny feeling moving in to a house that sat empty for so long. Was it . . . spooky?"

Mrs. Lee laughed and shook her head. "The only thing scary was all the repair work we had to do! The house was in quite a state when we bought it. There was even a family of raccoons living in the attic!"

Clio forced a laugh. "Well, I guess that's better than anything supernatural!" She checked for a reaction out of the corner of her eye, but Mrs. Lee seemed relaxed and unconcerned.

"Mm-hmm," Mrs. Lee said absently, turning onto Clio's street. The conversation was going nowhere, and Clio was running out of time.

"So it's good that nobody ever saw anything . . . strange . . . happen, huh?"

Mrs. Lee laughed as she pulled in front of Clio's house. "Oh, I don't know. It sure would make a good story if someone did, wouldn't it?"

. . . . .

The following morning, Clio and her aunt had a large platter of doughnuts ready when the other girls showed up. Clio stood anxiously behind the counter, dressed carefully in a belted paisley-patterned shift dress over black tights. Her bright green cardigan was buttoned just so, and her twist-out was pulled into a high puff on top of her head.

"Wow, this is really becoming a tradition," Maggie said. She picked up a chocolate frosted doughnut and took a huge bite. "I think I like it. So what's the big emergency, anyway?" She sat down cross-legged and tugged at her emoji-print leggings.

Tanya nibbled at a maple glazed, holding it delicately in a napkin. Rebecca sat beside her, dressed in a cropped boyfriend sweater over a plaid shirt-dress and balancing her blueberry-crumble dough-nut on a small plate. Kawanna, in a plain black fitted tee and baggy gray Juilliard sweats, perched next to the counter with a tall mug of chai tea.

Clio's chocolate-coconut doughnut sat forgotten on her plate. She was too nervous to eat. She knelt down on the floor, her hands twisting together in her lap. "You guys, I think the portal to the Night-mare Realm might still be open."

"What do you mean?" Rebecca asked.

Clio told them about the pantry, the silver-ware, the chandelier, and the ball. "I mean, if just one of those things had happened, it could have been an accident, or me being forgetful, or some-thing normal. But all together? And what about the ball? I threw it in the trash can myself!"

Rebecca put down her plate. "But we saw the portal seal. We checked it! How would it be open again?"

"It was a pretty intense scene out there, with the ice and everything," Maggie said. "I don't think the portal would go to all that trouble just to say, 'Hey, by the way, I'm still open!'"

Clio shrugged. "It seemed sealed to me, too, but I don't know what else it could be. Maybe something came out before the portal closed." She shook her head. "But whatever it is, there's *something* in that house."

"Minna's not acting strange, is she?" Rebecca asked, chewing on a blue-painted thumbnail. Her shaggy bangs fell forward, obscuring her face.

"No, she's totally fine," Clio said. "No one in the family seems to have noticed anything."

Tanya's brown eyes were thoughtful. "Maybe whatever's in the Plunkett Mansion has nothing to do with the portal. Maybe it's something else entirely."

Kawanna put down her tea. "That's an interesting idea."

Rebecca picked up her doughnut again. "You mean some other kind of supernatural being?"

Tanya ran her fingers through her bangs, making them stand straight up. "I was thinking more like a weird magnetic field around the house or something that would move stuff around." She pushed up the sleeves of her MATH CAMP sweatshirt and gazed at the ceiling, considering.

Clio folded her arms. "I don't think a magnetic field can cut paper dolls out of napkins, or take a ball out of a closed cabinet and carry it to the top of the stairs!"

Maggie licked the chocolate frosting off her fingers. "Good point."

"There's only one thing I can think of that would do that," Clio continued. She looked at her aunt Kawanna and nodded.

"A ghost."

"Not ghosts again," Tanya groaned. "I told you; that stuff is all fake. Houdini proved it!"

"Well, it didn't feel fake to me," Clio retorted.

Kawanna stood up and held out her hands. "Keep cool, girls. We don't know for sure what's going on yet." She walked over to the bookshelves and started stacking books on the counter. "We can start with research. Clio, you and Maggie are Team Ghost. Study the town's history. See what you can find out about the Plunkett family."

Clio and Maggie stood up, and Kawanna dumped a load of books in each girl's arms. "Tanya, you and Rebecca try to form a few other theories about what could be happening at the Plunkett Mansion."

Tanya opened her mouth, but Kawanna held up a finger. "See if you can come up with an experiment to determine if there's a scientific explanation, a supernatural one, or both." She piled books into Tanya's and Rebecca's arms. "Now, that should satisfy everyone."

"What about you, Auntie? What are you going to do?" Clio asked.

Kawanna balanced a few doughnuts on a plate and headed toward the back of the store. "You think this store runs itself? I have paperwork to do! Unlike you doughnut-eating freeloaders, some of us have real jobs." She winked at the girls and retreated into her office.

Maggie looked at the tower of dusty books in front of her and sighed. "I always imagined ghost-busting would be more fun than this."

Clio laughed. "Is that what we're doing? Busting ghosts?"

"Sure. Why not? In the movies they had these cool ray-gun things, and they zapped up ghosts, like some kind of laser vacuum." She called across the shop to Tanya, who already had her nose buried in a book. "How about it, T? You think you could make us some ghost-vacuum ray guns?"

Without raising her eyes from her book, Tanya slid a pencil out of the pocket of her backpack and underlined something. "Definitely not." Beside her, Rebecca typed notes on a silver laptop, her eyes sliding back and forth between the screen and the open book in front of her.

Clio skimmed the index of a book called *Piper: An Illustrated History*. Maggie peered over her shoulder and pointed halfway down the page, knocking into Clio's shoulder. "Look! The Plunkett Mansion!"

"Yeah, Maggie, I know. That's what I was looking for." Seeing Maggie's hurt expression, Clio tried to sound more encouraging. "Listen, we'll cover more ground if you go through your pile and I go through mine. Here. What about this?" She picked up the book at the top of Maggie's stack and handed it to her.

Maggie opened the book and groaned at the small print filling the page. "Ugh! Too boring!" Clio raised an eyebrow, and Maggie relented. "Fine, okay! Researching." She bent her head over the book but stood up a moment later.

"Maggie . . . ," Clio said.

"Relax, I'm just getting a pen!" Maggie walked slowly over to the counter and lingered over the pens in the cup beside the cash register. She tested each one on a small pad of paper she found under the counter. Feeling Clio's eyes on her, she stopped. "I was just seeing if she had a purple one."

Clio held up her hands. "Fine. Whatever." She went back to her book.

Maggie walked across the room and flopped down on the floor with a loud sigh. The shop was quiet for a while.

Across the room, Tanya and Rebecca conferred in soft voices, each pointing to a sketch that Tanya had made. "Looks like they're having fun, at least," Maggie muttered. Clio ignored her.

Maggie looked back down at her book, absently clicking her pen. She felt Clio's eyes on her. "What?" Clio's eyes moved to the pen. "Oh. Sorry," she said.

A few minutes later, Maggie began to hum, her eyes skimming the page. Soon, the humming turned to singing, her pen clicking in time with the melody.

Clio put down her pencil. "Maggie! Seriously!"

"Sorry!" Maggie said. "This book was really boring, so I was just singing the words to try to make it more interesting. There's, like, nothing in here."

"Then choose another book," Clio said slowly, pointing to the pile in front of Maggie.

"Fine. I will." Maggie pulled out the thinnest book in the pile and opened it up. She put it down in disgust. "Ugh! This one's even worse. It's in cursive!"

"Cursive?" Clio picked it up and read the inside cover. "Whoa! This is a diary. I think it must have belonged to the lady who owned the shop before. It's really old." She turned to a page in the middle. "*November 9, 1950. Tonight I went on a date with Stanley Wilson. It was boring and his breath was terrible. If he asks me out again I will tell him no.* Well, never mind; that's probably not going to tell us much."

Maggie's eyes lit up and she grabbed it out of Clio's hands. "Wait, Clio! You never know! There could be really important stuff in here. Maybe

Bad Breath Stanley has some spooky secrets to reveal!" She stretched out on her stomach with the open diary in front of her and bent her knees, her rhinestone-studded flats dangling from her toes. Clio smiled and went back to her own book.

A short time later, Maggie sat up. "You guys! Listen to this! *May 22, 1951. Tonight I went out again with Butch. I told my mom I was meeting Sally at the library, and Butch picked me up on the corner on his motorcycle. Sally said Butch was dangerous, but I told her she just doesn't understand him.*"

Clio's voice was patient. "Maggie, what does this have to do—"

"Just wait," Maggie said. "Listen." She held up the book and started reading again. "*Butch took me to the Plunkett Mansion! It's really creepy at night. Old Lady Plunkett was asleep, so we snuck down to her pond. There's this cool old gazebo down there called a folly. We sat and talked in it for a while, and then Butch showed me the Plunkett family cemetery. It was so spooky! Can you imagine burying your family in your own backyard?*"

Clio's eyes widened. "Wait a minute, the Plunkett Mansion has a cemetery?"

"Yup. And listen to this: *Butch told me the creepiest story while we were out there. He said that somebody drowned in the pond a long time ago, and it was so deep they never found the body. Butch swears that when he went swimming there once he felt something grab his leg and try to pull him under. I got so scared that I made him take me home after that.*" She put down the book and looked around the room triumphantly. "But she thinks she'll go out with him again if he asks her. At least he doesn't have bad breath."

"Did you hear that, guys?" Clio asked. "They never found a body! Don't ghosts sometimes haunt stuff because they want their body found?"

Tanya lifted her head from her book. "It's just an urban legend." The other girls looked at her blankly. "Every town has a story like that. The stories aren't true; they're just great stories that people *want* to be true. Look, I'll show you." She picked up Rebecca's laptop and typed *"urban legend pond drowned"* into the browser bar. There were 272,000 results. "See?"

Clio shrugged. "Well, just because it's an urban legend in some places doesn't mean it wasn't true here in Piper."

"Yeah, but we can't just take Butch's word for it.

We'd need to know for sure if it's based on a factual event," Tanya said. "If it did happen, there would have been a newspaper article about it somewhere, or an obituary or something. It would have to be sometime before that diary entry, and probably long enough before that it would be a legend and not something people in town really remembered themselves. So maybe sometime before 1940 or so, I'm guessing."

Clio searched her memory. "And it would have to be after 1892. That's when the house was built."

Rebecca groaned and pulled her dark gray beanie down over her eyes. "So, that just means we need to read through about fifty years of old newspapers."

"Well, don't look at me," Maggie said. "I'm terrible at that stuff. I got a C on my dance-history paper for Dance Elective. Dance Elective!" Maggie nudged Clio's shoulder. "You love history. Maybe you could use it for your fellowship project. You know, kill two birds with one stone?"

"I never understood what that expression is supposed to mean," Tanya said. "Who wants to go around killing birds?"

Clio picked up her backpack and stood up. "I guess I'm headed to the library. But there's no way I'm doing this by myself. Come on, Maggie. Grab your stuff, and I'll tell my aunt where we're going."

Maggie's eyes widened. "Me? I just told you I got a C on a dance paper! Do you really think I'm the best person for the job?"

Clio grinned. "Not really, but Rebecca and Tanya are busy with their own research, so you're pretty much the only person for the job." She held out her hand and helped Maggie up off the floor. "Let's go."

CHAPTER 11

CLIO LOVED THE Piper Town Library. It was a stately marble building with columns in the front, built back in the early 1900s, when Piper had been a lumber boomtown. The main reading room had high, arched ceilings and tiled marble floors that made Clio feel like she was walking into a cathedral of knowledge. She took a deep breath, imagining that she was inhaling every word of the books that surrounded her.

Clio waved hello to her favorite librarian, Mrs. Idelfonso, as she led Maggie past the main desk and down the stairs to a room filled with row after row of tall shelves crowded with books. The low ceilings and dim lighting made the space seem almost cavelike, and nooks in the walls held small wooden desks with green-shaded lamps.

The girls wove through the maze of bookshelves until they reached the central desk. The nameplate on the counter said ALISON UNDERWOOD. The pale woman behind it had dark hair pulled into a messy bun on top of her head with a pen tucked into the knot of hair. She had a mug of coffee and an open laptop in front of her, and she was reading a leather-bound book with a dark brown cover.

"Look!" Maggie said, pointing at the nameplate. "Underwood! Do you think she's related to Ethan? Maybe she talks to ghosts, too!"

"Shhh!" Clio whispered.

The woman still hadn't looked up. After a moment Clio cleared her throat, and the woman raised her eyes from the book. She took off her tortoiseshell reading glasses, and Clio noticed her eyes were a vivid blue.

"I'm sorry, I hope you weren't standing there too long before I noticed you. I'm working on my PhD, so I try to grab every moment I can to tackle my dissertation," she explained. "Hardly anyone comes down here, so I tend to get pretty absorbed." She waved one hand at the work on her desk. "Anyway, how may I help you?"

"Hi, Ms. Underwood. My name's Clio, and this is Maggie. We're hoping to take a look at old issues of the *Piper Register*."

"Of course!" Ms. Underwood replied. "All the past issues are on microfilm. What years are you looking for?"

Clio bit her lip. "Between 1892 and 1940, I think."

Ms. Underwood blinked. "That'll certainly keep you busy. Good thing there are two of you! Anything I can do to help you narrow it down?"

"Maybe," Clio said. "I'm researching the Plunketts, one of the town's founding families."

"It's for the Student Fellowship project at Sanger Middle," Maggie interjected proudly. "She's applying."

"Oh," Ms. Underwood said. "That's my son's school. Another Sanger student was here earlier, too. He should still be around somewhere."

Maggie leaned over the desk. "We may know him. What did he look like?"

Ms. Underwood thought for a moment. "Tall. Floppy blond hair. Braces."

Maggie suppressed an excited smile. "Sounds like it must be Trent," she said. Clio fought the urge to groan. It was hard enough keeping Maggie focused. With Trent there, too, it would be impossible to get anything done.

"The microfilm machines are kept in the stacks downstairs," Ms. Underwood explained. "There's no librarian down there, so I'll get you set up." She led Clio and Maggie down the staircase to a heavy fire door and pulled it open to reveal a long, low-ceilinged room that stretched the entire length of the library. It was almost completely dark, punctuated by the occasional red glow of an emergency-exit light. Ms. Underwood stepped between two tall shelves of books, and the fluorescent lights flickered on above her, following her movement down the aisle. "The lights are on motion sensors," she explained. "It helps save electricity. So if you suddenly find yourself sitting in the dark, just stand up and the lights should come on again."

After bringing Clio and Maggie to the microfilm-viewing machines, Ms. Underwood disappeared to pull the newspaper files the girls had requested, and the echo of her footsteps slowly faded until the girls heard the heavy fire door open and slam closed again. Maggie stood up behind the table and peered across the gloom of the empty basement. "It's kind of spooky down here, don't you think?"

Clio nodded. "A little. I'm glad you came with me. I definitely wouldn't want to be down here alone."

Ms. Underwood soon reappeared with a stack of small boxes in her arms. She turned on the two machines on the table and pulled one box from the top of the stack and one box from the bottom. "I thought you girls might have an easier time of it if you start from opposite ends of the year span. Who wants to start from 1892?"

"I will," Clio said, thinking of the photo she had seen in the dining room of the Lees' house. Ms. Underwood pulled out the tray of Clio's machine and slid a spool of film onto a spindle. She busied herself preparing the film until there, on the machine's magnified screen, was an image of the *Piper Register* for the week of January 3, 1892.

Clio whistled appreciatively. "I still can't get

over the fact that I can read a newspaper from over 120 years ago! It's the coolest!"

"Oh, I can definitely think of cooler things," Maggie said.

"Well, Clio, I guess not everyone loves history quite as much as we do," Ms. Underwood said with a wink. She threaded the 1940 spool into Maggie's machine and showed the girls how to use the buttons to control the film.

"Is your son Ethan Underwood, by chance?" Maggie asked.

"I should have figured that you might know each other from school," Ms. Underwood said. "Come to think of it, I've heard him mention a Clio now and then. Are you friends of his?"

Maggie looked over at Clio and tried to hide a smile. "So, he's mentioned Clio, huh? What did he say?"

"We have a few classes together," Clio said, kicking Maggie under the table. "He came into my auntie's costume shop the other day to put up a flyer for his business."

"Yeah, how's his business going, anyway? Has

he gotten any interesting new customers?" Maggie asked, raising her eyebrows at Clio.

Ms. Underwood looked between the two girls. "Ah. I see he told you about the Stalcup Gift, huh?" Seeing their nonplussed expressions, Ms. Underwood continued. "My side of the family is descended from the Stalcup line. Both the Stalcups and the Underwoods were among the founding families of Piper, but my mother's family is most known for its work as spiritualists, or mediums. During the old days of vaudeville, my ancestors' spiritualism shows would sell out entire theaters. Some of my relatives even held private séances for the rich and famous, including a few US presidents."

"So their powers were real?" Maggie asked. "People can really talk to ghosts?"

"Well, I never could," Ms. Underwood said. "But my grandmother used to tell me stories about when she was a little girl. She would be playing and look up to find spirits standing in her room like regular people. She would ask the ghosts what they wanted, but they never answered." She smiled to herself. "I remember hearing those stories as a little girl and hoping *so hard* that I wouldn't have the Stalcup Gift. My grandmother was always matter-of-fact about it, but I knew that I never, ever wanted to see a ghost."

"But Ethan has?" Maggie asked.

"Only Ethan knows for sure." Ms. Underwood gave a mysterious smile and walked away, leaving the girls alone.

CHAPTER 12

CLIO AND MAGGIE sat side by side, scrolling through page after page of old newspapers. It was tedious work, but Clio was starting to get the hang of it, skimming for the word *Plunkett*. She found stories about lumber mills, county fair prizes, births, and weddings, but nothing about any deaths or accidents at the pond. Maggie had her earbuds in, and Clio could hear the bass line as Maggie nodded her head in time with the music.

And then Clio found it.

Tragedy at Plunkett Pond, the headline screamed. Clio quickly scanned the article. She tapped Maggie on the shoulder. "Psst! Maggie!"

Maggie took out one earbud, her eyes still on the screen in front of her. "Huh?"

"Maggie! I found it!" Clio pointed at her screen. "T. D. Plunkett, the guy who built the Plunkett Mansion, had twin daughters, Harriet and Eudora, and a young son, Peter. In August 1895, while Mrs. Plunkett was putting Peter down for his nap, the twins went down to the pond to cool off. They were just going to wade in, but Eudora slipped and fell into the deeper water. Her sister ran for help, but by the time they got back to the pond, it was too late. She was only eight."

"That's horrible," Maggie said. "Did they ever find her body?"

"It doesn't say."

The two girls sat in silence for a moment. "You know," Maggie said, "the *idea* of ghosts seems so scary and exciting, but I never really thought about how every ghost means that someone died somewhere. It's actually super sad. Poor Eudora."

Clio nodded. Above their heads, the lights blinked out. "I'll stand up to turn them on again," Maggie said.

"Hold on," Clio answered, her hand on Maggie's

arm. At the other end of the floor, the aisle farthest from the stairwell, the fluorescent lights blinked on. "There's someone back there."

Then the lights of the next aisle came on. Then the next.

"I bet it's Trent," Maggie whispered, sounding excited. "He's probably been spying on us."

Clio's stomach twisted. "But what if it's not?"

The lights above each row of shelves came flickering on, closer and closer, until the last light flickered on just before their row.

No one came out.

Clio stood up, lighting up the ceiling overhead. "Who's there?"

There was a scuffling sound, and a few books fell off a shelf and onto the floor.

"Come on, Trent. It's not funny," Maggie said, standing up. "We're trying to get work done." She grabbed Clio's wrist and dragged her over to the row of bookshelves. "We're not scared, so you may as well just come out."

Clio and Maggie poked their heads around the shelf, half expecting to see Trent hunched over and snickering behind the rows of books.

There was no one there.

The girls looked at each other. "Okay, a ghost in the old Plunkett Mansion is one thing, but there's no way there's one in the library, too," Maggie said. "It's got to be Trent trying to scare us." Her voice lowered. "Right?"

"Maybe we should split up and search," Clio suggested half-heartedly, hoping Maggie would say no.

Maggie folded her arms. "You know how I feel about splitting up." Clio breathed an inward sigh of relief. "But I think you're right," Maggie continued. "Otherwise, whoever's down here can just sneak past us to the exit while we're on the other side of the room. Besides, I'm sure it's just Trent, anyway."

"Sure, okay, great. Let's definitely split up, then." Clio looked down the long rows of bookshelves. "So glad I suggested it," she mumbled to herself. Maggie was notoriously stubborn; it figured that the one time she would decide to agree with Clio was the one time that Clio didn't want her to.

The two girls split up to cover the exits on either

side of the floor. Clio slowly and methodically checked each aisle; her footsteps sounded lonely in the empty space until she heard Maggie moving on the opposite end.

"Any luck?" Clio asked.

"Nothing yet," Maggie called back.

Clio continued slowly down the aisles, searching for anything unusual. She thought she saw something move out of the corner of her eye, but when she turned to look, everything was still.

Finally, she reached an aisle just a few rows away from the microfilm machines. There was a small scattering of books on the floor. Clio remembered the sound she had heard earlier. She looked around her, then bent to gather the books that had fallen. Just as she was about to pick them up, she paused and looked closer. "Maggie! Come here!" She heard Maggie's footsteps hurrying toward her and watched her friend's red curls appear and disappear as she passed through the rows of bookcases.

"What is it?" Maggie asked breathlessly.

"Look." Clio pointed at a smudge of green that streaked one of the books on the ground. Her eyes scanned the shelves to find the empty spot where

the books had been. There was a streak of green on the bookshelf, too. Clio pointed. "And over there."

"That's not . . . moss, is it?" Maggie asked quietly, and the two girls looked uneasily at each other.

"I don't know," Clio whispered. She thought about how loud their footsteps had been as they walked the floor. And how they hadn't heard any footsteps at all when the lights had begun turning on by themselves.

BOOM.

The fire door slammed shut with a bang.

Clio and Maggie raced toward the exit and threw open the door. The stairwell was empty.

But stuck to the wall by the doorway was a blood red maple leaf.

CHAPTER
13

THE NEXT MORNING at school, Clio absentmind-edly turned the combination on her locker; her thoughts were still swirling around the events of the day before. She and Maggie had filled in the others when they'd gotten back from the library, but everyone seemed to have a different idea about what it all meant. By the end of the day, nobody was any closer to figuring out a plan for what to do next.

After what she had read in the *Register*, Clio was almost certain that there was a ghost in the Lees' house. But what about the green smudges and the leaf in the library? The last time she had seen something like that, it had led them straight to the Nightmare Realm, but her friends were certain they had sealed the portal for good. Could there be a connection between the ghost and the Nightmare Realm? There was only one person Clio could think of who might know. She had to talk to Ethan.

She found him in the hall later that morning before study hall. He was wearing a faded Star Wars T-shirt and jeans and knelt by his backpack, putting a few heavy books in his locker. Clio wiped her suddenly sweaty hands on the sides of her yellow wool color-block dress and fluffed her Afro puffs. Why was she so nervous?

Ethan was just zipping up his pack when Clio tapped him on the shoulder. "Hey, Ethan, um, can I talk to you about something?"

Ethan looked up, and his expression brightened when he saw Clio. "Oh, hey! Yeah, sure. I mean, definitely."

Clio bit her lip. "It's kind of . . . weird."

"That's cool; I like weird." He blushed and looked down at his shoes, a pair of gray Chuck

Taylors that he had drawn all over with black pen. "I have free period in the art studio. You wanna talk there?"

"Okay." Clio followed Ethan into the art studio. Every inch of wall space was filled with pen-and-ink drawings and watercolor paintings, turning the room into a patchwork quilt of dizzying colors and patterns. Shelves were crammed with ceramic projects in various states of completion, and paper mobiles cascaded from the ceiling. Easels with blank canvases were set up in one corner, and a few older students worked at a long table in the back of the room. They looked up and waved when they saw Ethan walk in.

Ethan slid a black portfolio from a set of low, flat shelves and pulled out a sheet of heavy paper. He laid it on a nearby table and grabbed a dusty gray jar of drawing pencils. Clio glanced down at the page. "Whoa, is that a raven?" The sketch was still rough, but Clio could already tell that it was good.

"I started it yesterday." Ethan sat down. "Is it okay if I work while we talk?"

"Of course," Clio said.

Ethan slid a sheet of blank paper across the table. "Here. You can draw something, too." He moved the jar of pencils closer.

Clio picked up a pencil and looked down at the blank page. "So you really do believe in ghosts, right?"

Ethan blinked. "Well, duh. That's like asking me if I believe in dogs. Or the sun."

Clio drew a small spiral in the corner of her paper. Her pencil moved, and the spiral became a ram's horn. "Okay. But do you believe in other stuff, too?" she asked without looking up.

Ethan's brow furrowed. "What kind of other stuff?"

The ram's horn grew into a crown, and Clio found herself drawing hair cascading out of it. The hair was jointed, like spiders' legs. "Like, I guess, you know . . . other realms and creatures and things like that."

Ethan thought for a moment. "My great-grandma Moina was always writing about the Spirit Realm, so I don't see why there can't be other realms, too."

Clio sighed with relief. "Okay. Good. Then this

is going to sound way less out there to you. Because my friends and I have visited one of those other realms: the Nightmare Realm."

Ethan dropped his pencil and leaned forward. "Tell me everything."

$$\cdots\cdots$$

When the bell finally rang at the end of the period, Clio and Ethan looked up, startled. Their drawings lay forgotten on the table, and the older kids were long gone.

"Oh, shoot. I have to get to math!" Clio grabbed her backpack and threw it over her shoulder. She turned to Ethan. "I gotta go. Um . . . thanks for listening. I know how it sounds, but I swear, it really did happen."

Ethan reached out and touched Clio's arm. "Hey, Clio?" He blushed.

"Yeah?"

"I believe you."

CHAPTER 14

AFTER SCHOOL THAT day, the four girls met up at Creature Features. Clio was still thinking about her conversation with Ethan. It had been nice to talk about it with someone else. Someone who truly believed in ghosts.

Kawanna gave her niece a big hug. "You look like you've had a day, Li'l Bit." Clio rested her head against her aunt's arm.

"Yeah," she said. "It was a day. But I think it ended up okay."

"Good," Kawanna said, rubbing her back. "Now, have you girls decided what the plan is for the Plunkett Mansion?"

Tanya and Rebecca looked at each other. "We finalized it during study hall today," Rebecca said. "The first thing we need to do is to observe and record exactly what kind of paranormal stuff is happening at the Lees', and when. Maybe if we can find a pattern behind it, that will help us figure out what's causing it."

Tanya rubbed her hands together, her brown eyes sparkling. "So we're gonna do a stakeout."

Maggie's face brightened. "A stakeout? Cool! Do we get to wear disguises?"

"Why would we wear disguises?" Rebecca asked. "Clio's *supposed* to be there."

"Well, what about the rest of us?" Maggie asked.

Tanya pulled out a hand-drawn map of the house. "Clio is babysitting for the Lees on Wednesday night, right before they leave for their trip on Thursday. Their wedding anniversary is right after they get back in town, the same night that Clio's going to see *Hamilton* in Portland with her parents. Since they asked Clio about a backup sitter, she can bring Rebecca along on Wednesday to meet the family." She pointed to a small X on the map. "Kawanna will wait with Maggie and me just down the road, and after the Lees leave, she'll drop us off. We'll set up a perimeter outside the house and watch for anything unusual."

Maggie shimmied her shoulders. "Oooh, 'set up a perimeter' sounds so official. I like it!"

Kawanna and the girls bent their heads over the map and put the final steps of their plan in place.

· · · · ·

Two days later, Clio and her friends met outside the shop just after sunset. The weather had turned chilly, so Clio zipped up her vintage moto jacket and wrapped a chunky oversize wool scarf around her neck. "I should have changed into jeans," she moaned, shivering in her opaque black tights and short plaid skirt. She pulled her slouchy black beanie lower over her ears.

"You should have just dressed for a stakeout, like me," Maggie said. She wore a fake fur vest on top of an oversize black sequined sweater and black leggings. Leopard-print high-tops and bright fuchsia socks completed the look.

Tanya shrugged into her black hoodie. "Definitely stakeout-ready, Mags. Especially the socks."

"What can I say?" Maggie said. "I'm just chic like that."

Kawanna pulled her turquoise Scout around the corner, and the girls gathered their things and threw them in the cargo area before sliding into the bench seats.

When they pulled into the Lees' driveway a few minutes later, Kawanna kissed the top of Clio's head. "Shoot Maggie and Tanya a text a few minutes after the Lees leave and you and Rebecca get settled with Minna. Then I'll drive them back over, and they'll take their positions outside. Don't worry; we're just around the corner."

A short time later, the Lees drove off, and Maggie and Tanya were soon in place outside. Rebecca and Clio sat with Minna at the kitchen table as she finished her dinner of fish sticks and carrots. "So, Minna, are you excited for your trip tomorrow?" Clio asked.

Minna nodded. "We're gonna see my grandma." She smiled. "She loves me, and we play lots of games!"

"That sounds really fun," Rebecca said. "Is Wesley coming, too?"

Minna shook her head. "We're going on an airplane. So Mom says he has to stay home." She peeped under the table, where Wesley was lying at her feet, and slipped him a fish stick. The dog took it gently from her fingers. "Dad says don't worry, because somebody's taking care of him." Minna looked tearful.

"I know you'll miss him a lot, but it's only for a few days," Clio said reassuringly.

"You'll be back before you know it," Rebecca added. "Hey! It looks like you're almost finished eating! What would you like to play after dinner?"

Minna munched thoughtfully on her last carrot. After a moment, her face brightened. "Hide-and-seek," she said. Rebecca's and Clio's eyes met above Minna's head. Hide-and-seek was the last thing Clio wanted to do.

Clio picked up Minna's dinner dishes and carried them over to the sink. She raised her voice so the little girl could hear her across the room. "I don't know, Minna; maybe we should play hide-and-seek another time."

"Pleeeease?" Minna drew out the word, her brown eyes pleading.

"I have an idea," Rebecca suggested. "Maybe we could do an art project!"

Minna folded her arms, a scowl darkening her face. "I don't want to do art. I want to play hide-and-seek."

Rebecca shrugged and looked at Clio. *What should we do?* her expression seemed to ask.

Clio rinsed the dishes and put them in the dishwasher, thinking. Finally, she turned back to face Minna. "I guess we could play for a little while, but no hiding upstairs or in the basement. Only on the first floor."

Minna's eyebrows lowered. "I don't like the basement. It's too scary! I won't hide there."

"Good," Clio said. "Rebecca will hide with you, okay? And I'll look for you both."

"Okay," Minna said, her scowl gone. She stood up. "Close your eyes and count to one hundred."

Clio covered her eyes and started counting. She heard Rebecca and Minna creep out of the room. Keeping her head down, she sent a quick text to Maggie.

OMG WE ARE PLAYING HIDE
AND SEEK

?!? why would you do that?

Minna really wants to

LMK if anything weird
happens. quiet out here so far

ttyl

Clio lifted her head and listened. She was hoping that Wesley might give her a clue to find the two girls, but he was curled up in his bed, his eyes droopy. She poked around the TV room, pushing the floor-length drapes back from either side of the window and peeking behind the couch. Nothing there.

The next obvious hiding spot was the pantry. Clio steeled herself and turned the knob, pushing sharply inward. The door flew open, banging into the bag of dog food against the wall. *Definitely not stuck anymore*, Clio thought. With one foot in the doorway, Clio switched on the pantry light and dragged the bag to prop the door open. She checked under the shelves and behind a pile of plastic storage bins. No one was hiding, and Clio wasn't sure whether to feel disappointed or relieved. The pantry made Clio nervous enough; she definitely would have screamed to find someone hiding in there, even though she was expecting it.

The dining room was next. Clio lingered in the doorway, looking nervously at the dark room. The chandelier was silent and still. She switched on the light. There weren't many places to hide in here, she was relieved to see. She crouched to peer under the table. Empty. She felt a slight breeze move across the floor, and goose bumps broke out on her arms. The chandelier tinkled, and Clio stood up quickly. It grew quiet again.

The credenza under the mirror had large cabinet doors. It was certainly big enough to fit Minna, and maybe Rebecca, too. Clio tugged at the tarnished brass handles of the carved doors. The hinges creaked as they slowly opened, and a musty smell seeped out of the wood. Clio coughed. Inside was a pile of faded table linens and a crystal punch bowl. Clio closed the cabinet doors again.

Leaving the dining room light on, she entered the living room. There was no light switch on the wall, and Clio stood silhouetted in the doorway, her eyes struggling to make out the faint shapes of furniture in the dark room. Her shadow loomed before her, blacking out the rectangle of light that stretched across the floor.

Clio had never been in the living room, and it took her a moment to find a floor lamp to switch on. Its warm amber glow was just bright enough to illuminate a high-backed leather chair and a round rosewood table. *This could be a nice spot for reading, I bet.* Clio smiled wryly. *If the house wasn't haunted, anyway.* She crossed the room to an old piano with brittle, yellowed sheet music still sitting on the music stand. She switched on a painted porcelain lamp on top of the piano, but the extra light made little difference; the corners of the room were still bathed in shadow. Moth-eaten velvet drapes framed the front windows, and Clio checked for feet beneath the hems. "Nobody hiding here," she said loudly, in the hopes that Minna would giggle and give the girls away. The room was silent.

Clio navigated around the oval coffee table to check behind the tufted velvet sofa, her hands running over the polished wood of its curved edges. Above the sofa, sepia-toned photographs of the Plunkett family framed an oval convex mirror. Clio noticed that one of the pictures had been turned to face the wall. Why?

Clio picked up the photograph and drew in a sharp breath. It was a portrait of the Plunkett twins. They were a little older than in the dining room photo, and both pale-eyed girls wore dark dresses with petticoats and puffed sleeves. Each cradled a doll in her arms. Clio held the photo in her hands. *One of these poor girls never got the chance to grow up. She never even got to cuddle her doll again.* Filled with sadness, Clio gently dusted the glass front and replaced the portrait properly on the wall.

The portrait flew across the room and slammed into the opposite wall, glass shattering across the floor. Clio screamed.

In the hallway, the closet door flew open, and Rebecca and Minna tumbled out. "Are you all right?" Rebecca asked breathlessly.

"I—" Clio saw the frightened look on Minna's face. "Uh . . . I accidentally dropped a picture and the glass broke." She forced a smile, but her hands were shaking. "Silly me! Minna, why don't we start a movie for you, and Rebecca and I will clean this up. We'll come join you in a few minutes."

The girls settled Minna in the TV room, and Clio brought the broom and dustpan to the living room, where Rebecca was crouched over the broken photograph.

Rebecca held a small, cream-colored rectangle in her right hand. "Clio, I found something hidden behind the picture."

Clio leaned forward to see. "What is it?"

Rebecca's eyes were wide. "It's an old calling card. From Ethan's great-grandma Moina."

CHAPTER
15

CLIO SWITCHED OFF the overhead light in Minna's room and walked out quietly, leaving the door slightly ajar and the girl sound asleep in her bed. Luckily, Minna hadn't noticed anything was wrong, despite Clio's phone buzzing all night from the flurry of texts between Rebecca and the others.

As she walked down the hall, she slipped her phone out of her pocket and skimmed through the texts between her friends. The last two from Maggie and Tanya caught her eye.

Something on the porch.

> Gonna check it out.

By the time Clio got to the bottom of the stairs, Rebecca was nowhere to be found. "Rebecca!" Clio called softly. There was no answer. Clio picked up her phone and texted the group:

> Where's Rebecca?

No answer. Clio did a sweep of the first floor, scanning all the rooms, the closets, and the pantry. They were empty. Clio's voice rose with anxiety. "Rebecca?" The back door was locked and bolted from the inside. Where could she be? Had the ghost done something to her?

Finally her phone buzzed.

> Outside

Clio rushed to the front hall and paused by the door. She peered through the window, looking for the black-and-white stripes of Rebecca's cropped hoodie. The clock chimed out the hour, making Clio jump. She gritted her teeth. *What is with this stupid clock?* Clio thought. She checked the time on her phone: seven forty-five. But the clock was chiming eight. *It can't even get the time right!*

The front door was unlocked, and Clio opened it and stepped onto the porch. "Hey, you guys! What's going on?" She was yanked to the side, and a hand covered her mouth.

"Shhh!" Maggie whispered. "Don't scare it off!"

Clio turned to Maggie. *What?* she mouthed.

Maggie pointed to the other end of the porch, where a twisted creature was peering into the living room window, hanging from the shutters by its long, ropy arms. The creature's face was pressed against the glass, its head moving back and forth as though it was searching for something. It was completely unaware of Rebecca and Tanya, who were slowly closing in. The girls carried an old fishing net between them.

Rebecca and Tanya looked at each other and nodded their heads. They threw the net over the creature, who shrieked and struggled against the tangled rope. "Got it!"

Clio and Maggie ran across the porch. "What is it?"

Tanya grimaced and tried to restrain the wriggling creature. "I can't tell yet! It's too dark, and this thing won't stay still! Help!"

Clio grabbed a corner of the net and held it down. The creature's silhouette looked vaguely familiar. "I think this is what was following us in the woods when we closed the portal," she said. "It had that same kind of monkey shape, with those skinny long arms."

"Maggie," Tanya said, breathing heavily. "There's a flashlight in the pocket of my jacket. See if you can grab it while the rest of us hold the net."

The creature lunged against the net in violent bursts, the three girls struggling to keep it trapped. Maggie gingerly made her way around the chaotic scene and slipped her hand into Tanya's pocket. She pulled out the flashlight and clicked it on. "Let's see what's been causing so much trouble around here," she said, and shone the beam onto the animal. She gasped and almost dropped the light. "It's . . . it's that horrible thing!"

"What?" Clio asked. "What horrible thing?" The creature's strong legs were scratching and kicking against her, so she couldn't get a view of the face.

Rebecca stopped fighting the creature. "I can't believe it," she said. "It's the changeling."

CHAPTER
16

THE GIRLS DROPPED the net, and the changeling ceased its writhing. It bared its jagged teeth, hissing like a feral cat. Sunken eyes peered out at them malevolently from the pitted, decaying face. It was still wearing the onesie from when it had pretended to be Kyle, the baby Rebecca babysat. Long, sinewy arms snaked out from the rotted-log body, and mushroom-capped fingers reached through the net, snatching at the girls. Clio jumped back. An ugly giggle burbled out of the changeling, and it snapped its jaws together.

"I think it remembers you, Clio," Rebecca said.

"How does it remember anything?" Maggie

asked. "The last time we saw this digusto thing, it could barely limp its way through the portal out of the Nightmare Realm. I thought it was supposed to be dead!" The changeling swiped at Maggie with its taloned feet, and Maggie swatted it away. "Ugh! Why are you still alive, you nasty little monster?"

"Oh, don't be so mean," Rebecca said. "It can't help being horrible."

"I don't care if ol' Horrible here can help it or not; we almost got killed because of this little nightmare." Maggie scowled at the changeling.

"It wasn't his fault," Rebecca said. "Was it, Horrible?" The creature reached one mushroomed finger through the net and touched Rebecca's hand.

"Oh, so we're making friends with it now?" Maggie asked.

"Come on, Maggie," Rebecca said. "I took care of him for, like, weeks."

"Yeah, but that's only because you thought he was a baby!" Maggie retorted. She eyed the changeling critically. "Although I don't know how a person could confuse you with anything remotely pleasant, Horrible."

"Okay, guys, we figured out the mystery, so let's let him go," Rebecca said. She lifted a corner of the net and reached in to pull the changeling free.

Tanya grabbed her arm. "Let him go?" she asked, surprised. "But we need to know why he's been hanging around the Plunkett Mansion playing tricks, and why he was following us!"

"What difference does it make?" Maggie asked. "He can't tell us anything, anyway." As she spoke, a white grub dropped from the changeling and squirmed on the ground. Maggie shuddered. "I want this little yuckfest as far away as possible. Can't we just tell him to get lost and never come back?"

Tanya turned to Clio. "What do you think we should do?"

Clio looked through the front window, thinking. She could see the broken picture of the Plunkett twins on the living room floor, resting against the wall where she'd left it. "I don't know, but we should go back inside. I don't want to leave Minna in the house alone."

"We can't bring this thing inside. Look at him! He'll stink up the whole place!" Maggie said.

"Exactly," Rebecca said. The changeling snarled and squirmed under the net, and Rebecca's voice softened. "No offense, Horrible." She looked at the other girls. "What are we gonna do, take him prisoner? We can't do that. Where would we keep him? How would we feed him?"

"But we don't want him hurting anyone else," Tanya said. "He hurt you, remember?"

"But that was only because he was scared," Rebecca said. "You should understand that, T. You're always saying that animals only attack when they're afraid."

"But this isn't an animal," Tanya said. "We need to learn more about him before we let him go."

Clio looked anxiously at the front door. "I have to go check on Minna," she said. As soon as she stood up, Horrible wriggled out from under the net and darted between the other girls. He vaulted over the porch rail and disappeared into the night.

Tanya jumped up and followed Clio across the porch. "I can't believe you let him go. Don't you want to know what he was doing here?"

"I didn't let him go," Clio retorted. "I just stood up, okay?" She opened the front door. "I have to go inside."

Tanya followed her. "Clio, what's wrong?" The other girls crowded into the front hall behind her. There was a mechanical whirring sound behind them, and the clock struck again, the chimes booming through the house. The girls jumped.

Clio snarled. "I hate that thing!" She gave the clock a dark look, noticing the silvery white moon had moved across the clock's face. Clio shuddered. She didn't like the cold look in the moon woman's eyes.

"Wait here," Clio said. She headed to Minna's room, her mind going over all of the strange events that had happened in the house. Some of them could certainly have been caused by a mischievous changeling. But could all of them?

Minna was curled up in a tight little ball, her hair damp with sweat. It was cool in the room, and the bedcovers were light. Why was she so sweaty?

Clio smoothed her hair back and felt her forehead for fever. It didn't feel warm.

Minna rolled over and cried out in her sleep. Her eyes flew open and she sat up, frightened. Clio reached out to hold her. She watched Minna's face relax as she recognized her bedroom. Clio leaned in close and spoke in Minna's ear. "It's okay. You're safe. Did you have a bad dream?"

Minna nodded. "I was playing with my friends. It was fun. But someone tried to pull me in the water. She wouldn't let go!"

Clio's blood froze. She made her voice sound light and calm. "That sounds scary. I'm sure glad it was only a dream. Who were your friends?"

Minna shrugged. "I don't know their names. They were older than me."

"What did they look like?" Clio asked.

Minna thought for a moment. "They had yellow hair and wore dresses. They looked the same."

"Like . . . twins?"

Minna nodded again.

Clio tried to keep calm, but she felt fear rising

in her throat. She had never spoken about the Plunkett twins when she was babysitting, and Minna's parents didn't seem to know anything about the tragedy that had happened at the pond. How were the twins in Minna's dream? Had she noticed the photos downstairs? But that still didn't explain the water.

Minna relaxed against the pillow.

"Ready to go back to sleep?" Clio asked.

"Uh-huh."

Clio tucked the covers around the little girl. "Do you want me to stay with you?"

"Uh-huh." Minna's eyes were already closing.

There was no way she could leave Minna's side until her parents got home. Not after what Minna had told her. Clio took out her phone to text Rebecca.

minna had a bad dream.
staying w/her.

need any help?

im ok. lees will b home soon.

maggie and tanya heading out
ill finish cleaning up here

ask them 2 meet b4 school
tmrw

tanya sez CF at 7?

k

maggie sez 2 tell u she hates
this plan

lol tell her sorry
c u in a bit

Clio watched Minna sleep, still troubled by the little girl's dream. Could it really be just a coincidence?

Or was it a message?

CHAPTER 17

CREATURE FEATURES WAS far less festive at 7:00 a.m. The shop was dark when Clio and her friends arrived at the storefront. Clio used her key to unlock the door and hurried to the panel to switch off the alarm.

Maggie cast a crestfallen glance at the empty counter. "What? No doughnuts?"

Kawanna wandered in from the back and took a yawning sip from her mug of strong, steaming tea. "Too early."

"Auntie's more of a night owl than an early bird," Clio explained.

Rebecca grinned and reached into her backpack.

"Luckily, I have some muffins left over from Sunday's batch."

Maggie's face lit up. "Blueberry?"

Rebecca nodded. "Blueberry-lemon crumble."

Maggie sighed with relief. "You're a goddess!"

Rebecca laughed and shrugged. "I know."

Kawanna gestured to the hallway behind her. "I have some tea set up in my office." The girls dropped their backpacks against the counter and followed Clio's aunt into her cozy office at the back of the shop.

Clio loved Aunt Kawanna's office, with its bursting bookshelves, carved antique desk, and warm, sunset-colored walls. She squeezed into the peacock-blue velvet loveseat with Tanya and Rebecca; Maggie flopped into the worn leather armchair beside them and kicked off her fuchsia sequined flats. Kawanna laid the tea tray on the black lacquer coffee table and retreated to the gilded, thronelike chair behind her desk.

Kawanna broke off a piece of muffin and put the rest on a saucer. "So what do we know?"

Tanya poured herself a cup of tea. "We found Horrible a short time after Clio saw a photograph fly off the wall, so he must be involved somehow. I think he's been playing pranks over at the Plunkett Mansion, but we don't know why." She cast a sideways glance at Rebecca and Clio. "I wanted to find out more, but he *escaped* before we could question him."

"He can't even talk!" Rebecca shot back. "How were you planning to question him?"

"We would have thought of something," Tanya said. "At the very least, we could have found out if he was working for the Night Queen or not."

"Why would he be working for her?" Rebecca asked. "She tried to have him killed!"

"Then why was he hanging around the portal when we closed it?" Maggie asked. "Clio said she saw him in the woods that night."

The other girls looked at Clio. She nodded slowly. "It was too dark to see clearly, but I think it was Horrible following us that night."

Rebecca took a bite of her muffin. "There are lots of reasons that he could have been at the portal," she said with her mouth full. "Maybe he wanted to see it closed just as much as the rest of us did!"

"But it seems more likely that he's working for the queen," Tanya said. "Now that the portal is closed and the queen can't get through, she could be using Horrible as a way of getting back at us."

"But why the Lees' house, then?" Rebecca asked. "Why would Horrible go there, and not our houses? Or the shop?"

"That's a good question." Kawanna turned to the bookshelf behind her. "Let's think about what we know about changelings. The Night Queen made him, but things went a little haywire when he tried to go back to her. What happens when a changeling can't return to its maker?" She pulled out a few books.

"I don't remember reading anything about that," Tanya said. "I don't know if it's ever happened before."

"But wait a minute." Clio spoke hesitantly. "What if it's *not* Horrible that's haunting the Plunkett Mansion?" She heard the uncertainty in her voice and wished that Ethan was there to back her up.

"Come on, Clio; it has to be!" Tanya said. "Spooky things happen at the Plunkett Mansion.

We find Horrible there. That can't just be a coincidence!"

"But how would Horrible make a picture fly off the wall when he wasn't even in the room?" Clio challenged. "Is he, like, telekinetic all of a sudden?"

Tanya made a frustrated gesture. "Well, that's what I wanted to find out before you let him *escape*."

Clio sighed. "I didn't *let* him escape. I had to go inside to check on Minna. And it's a good thing I did, because she was having a bad dream. A dream about the Plunkett twins!"

Maggie's jaw dropped. "What?!"

"In the dream, one of them was trying to pull her underwater."

Maggie leaned forward in her chair. "No way!" she whispered.

Rebecca nodded grimly. "Clio told me last night before the Lees got home." Tanya opened her mouth to say something, but Rebecca held up her hand. "Just hear her out, okay?"

"Look, I know what you're going to say," Clio said, putting down her teacup. "Maybe the pictures in the house gave Minna ideas. Maybe she overheard someone telling the story somewhere. But I think something was trying to reach into her dreams, and it definitely wasn't Horrible."

The others stared at her, unsure of what to say. Rebecca looked sympathetic, but Maggie seemed uncertain. Tanya's skeptical expression could have been carved from stone. Kawanna just sipped her tea, patiently waiting for Clio to finish.

"There *is* a ghost in that house," Clio said firmly. "And I know how to prove it."

CHAPTER
18

THE NEXT NIGHT, the four girls stood on the dark porch outside the Plunkett Mansion again. Kawanna waved from the driveway and began backing the turquoise Scout down the narrow lane. "Text me when you're ready to be picked up, and stay safe!" she called from the open car window.

Clio waved and adjusted her gauzy blue scarf before ringing the bell.

"Why are you ringing the bell?" Maggie asked. "I thought the Lees were out of town."

"They are," Clio answered simply. She looked away, humming tunelessly, a small smile on her face.

Maggie narrowed her eyes. "Wait a second. You only do that humming thing when you're up to something. What's going on?"

A few moments later, Ethan opened the front door. "Hey, Clio. Right on time."

Clio grinned. "I told you we'd make it."

"Hold up," Tanya said. "What's he doing here?"

"Dogsitting," Ethan answered. Wesley stood next to him and looked up adoringly at the boy.

"You sure are," Clio said. "Wow!" Her voice glowed with admiration. "He doesn't even look at his own family like that! You really *do* have a way with animals."

Ethan shrugged, his ears turning pink. "I tried to tell you."

Clio looked up to find Maggie watching the two of them, her eyes sparkling with interest.

"Come on in," Ethan said, opening the door wider. Clio introduced the girls to Ethan, and they followed him down the front hall and into the kitchen. "I already took Wesley out and gave him his dinner. We were just having some chill time together."

"You're not staying here alone overnight, are you?" Maggie asked.

Ethan shook his head. "No, I'll catch a ride home with you guys later, and then come back in the morning to give him breakfast and a walk before school. He has a doggy door, so he can go out when I'm not here."

"Wow, that's really cool of you to take such good care of the Lees' dog," Maggie said, looking pointedly over at Clio. Her rhinestone bangles jangled down her arm.

Tanya sighed impatiently. "It's his job, Mags."

"Well, still," Maggie said, "lots of people wouldn't be that nice if it were their job. Don't you think so, Clio?"

Ethan shoved his hands into the pockets of his dark jeans and looked at the floor. "I guess I just really like animals."

Maggie nudged Clio. "Clio likes animals, too."

Tanya looked around at the other faces in the room. "I'm sorry, am I the only one who wants to know what we're doing here?"

Ethan pulled his hands out of his pockets and

scratched his nose. "Oh, I'm sorry. My bad. I thought Clio told you."

"Told us what?" Tanya asked.

Clio reached into her pocket. "I hired him to check the house for ghosts."

Tanya threw her arms up in the air. "Seriously? Ugh. Why am I not surprised?" She turned to Clio. "You're not really paying him for this, are you?" She turned back to Ethan. "No offense."

Clio pulled out a ten dollar bill and handed it to Ethan. "He gave me a discount 'cause I got him the dogsitting gig."

Ethan smiled at her and pocketed the money. "Anything for you, Clio." Maggie looked ready to burst.

"Listen, I know you guys think it's only Horrible, but I *know* there's something else in this house, and I told you I'd prove it," Clio said. "Ethan's a medium, so he's the best person to help us figure out what's going on with this ghost." She hesitated. "Well, he's kind of the only person." She looked at Ethan. "No offense."

"Wouldn't we be better off doing some more research than paying some charlatan to pretend to talk to ghosts?" Tanya asked. She turned to Ethan. "No offense."

"Just because something isn't scientifically proven doesn't mean it's not real," Clio countered.

"Yeah," Maggie said. "Let the man speak, Tanya."

Tanya put her hands on her hips. "Fine. Have you found any '*ghosts*'?" She held up her fingers to make air quotes around the word *ghost*.

"I haven't been able to talk to anything here yet, but I definitely feel some kind of presence," Ethan said, "and so does Wesley."

"How do you know that?" Tanya challenged.

Ethan shrugged. "He told me."

Tanya rolled her eyes. "Of course he did." She turned to Rebecca. "Are you buying any of this?"

Rebecca chewed on her thumbnail, thinking. "All I know is I was here when the picture flew off the wall, and I was here when Minna had a nightmare about the Plunkett twins," she said finally.

"Yeah, but did you actually *see* the picture fly off the wall?" Tanya asked.

"Well, no. I was in the closet with Minna," Rebecca mumbled.

"Exactly," Tanya said.

"Well, *I* saw it, and *I'm* the one who hired Ethan, so the least you can do is let me get my money's worth."

"Luckily that isn't much," Tanya mumbled under her breath. Everyone looked at her. "No offense," she said to Ethan.

Clio turned to Ethan and shook her head. "Sorry about her."

Ethan gave a tight smile. "It's okay. I've heard it all before. It kind of goes with the territory. Believe me, I've heard worse."

A guilty expression passed across Tanya's face, and her voice grew kinder. "I'm sorry; that was mean. Look, I may not believe in ghosts, but that doesn't give me the right to make fun of you." She held out her hand. "From now on, I promise to keep an open mind. Friends?"

Ethan grinned crookedly and shook her hand. "Friends."

"Now that we got that over with," Maggie said, "can we *please* hear about the spooky things Ethan's found out? I'm dying to know!"

"Yeah, come on," Rebecca said. "You've kept us in suspense long enough!"

"Well, I'm no expert," Ethan said. Tanya opened her mouth and quickly closed it again. "But there are plenty of reasons to believe there could be a ghost here."

"We found your great-grandma's card behind one of the portraits on the wall," Rebecca said. "Did she come here looking for ghosts, too?"

"She did." Ethan walked into the TV room and came back with a small wooden chest. "These are Great-Grandma Moina's files." He opened the chest, and a flood of yellowed papers and news clippings spilled out. "Sorry, I'm not great at being organized."

"Neither am I," Maggie said with a grin. The girls knelt on the floor next to Ethan and helped him clean up the mess.

Maggie picked up a newspaper clipping, the paper brittle with age. "Hey! Look at this!" She read the headline aloud: "*World-Famous Spiritualist Holds Séance for Prominent Local Spinster.*" Her green eyes were wide as she looked at Ethan and handed him the clipping.

Clio studied the article's photo. "Hey, that's the same picture you showed me at Creature Features! That was taken here?"

Ethan nodded. "When Harriet grew up, she invited my great-grandma to come here for a reading. See, when her sister, Eudora, died, their parents totally couldn't handle it. After the funeral, they thought the best thing to do was just pretend Eudora never existed. They put away all the pictures of her. If anyone brought up her name, her parents would just change the subject."

"That's terrible!" Rebecca said. "I would have lost it if my parents had done that when my Nai Nai died. I still sleep with the blanket she made me."

Ethan looked down, tracing the edges of the news clipping. "At the time, the parents thought they were doing the right thing. They figured it would make it easier for the family to move on to happier times." He stacked the clipping on top of a pile of papers. "She didn't speak about it while her parents were alive, but Harriet never got over her sister's death. She even refused to marry so that she would never have to leave her childhood home. Back in 1905, a guy asked Harriet to marry him. She said no, and when he asked her why, she said, 'Sisters can never be parted.'"

Maggie shuddered. "Whoa, that's kind of a creepy thing to say." Then she thought for a moment. "Wait, how do you know she said that?"

Ethan put the papers back into the chest and closed the lid. "Because the guy who asked Harriet to marry him was Owen Stalcup."

"Stalcup?" Clio asked. "So you mean—"

"Yup. Later that year he met and married Sally Lawrence, and my great-great-grandma Moina was their first child, born in 1906."

"And Harriet never dated anyone else? She just stayed here with her parents and her brother?" Maggie asked.

Ethan nodded. "After her younger brother was killed in World War I, she was their only remaining child. And as soon as Harriet's parents died, Harriet pulled everything left of Eudora out of the attic and hired my great-grandma to hold a séance to try to communicate with her."

"What happened? Did it work?" Rebecca asked.

Ethan looked uncomfortable. "That's the part I don't know. Those papers were lost."

"Lost?! Then how are we supposed to find out what happened?" Tanya asked.

Maggie nudged her. "I thought you didn't believe in ghosts."

"I didn't! I mean, I don't!" Tanya said quickly. "It's just, you know, it's a great story, and I want to know how it ends," she finished lamely.

"Uh-huh," Maggie said knowingly.

"There's only one way to find out if Moina was ever able to reach the ghost," Clio said.

"What is it?" Rebecca asked.

"We re-create the séance. Right here. Tonight."

CHAPTER
19

"I CAN'T BELIEVE I'm doing this," Tanya said. The five were seated around the dining room table, which Ethan and Clio had draped with a white cloth. Clio placed three candles in the middle of the table. In front of Ethan were a bell, a book, and a wooden mallet. Wesley lay curled up next to his chair, his gray muzzle buried under his paws.

"Aren't we going to use a Ouija board or something?" Rebecca asked. "I thought that's how people communicated with ghosts."

Ethan shook his head. "With a Ouija, everyone touches the planchette to move it around the board. That just leaves too much room for human error. Or cheating. If just one person wants to fake a ghost, they can manipulate the planchette and trick everyone else. Too messy. Too unscientific."

Tanya gave Ethan an approving glance. "Too many variables." She opened her notebook and pulled a pencil out of her jacket pocket.

Ethan smiled. "Exactly."

"Plus, whenever anybody uses a Ouija board in the movies, stuff goes *real* bad *real* fast," Maggie said.

"Should we maybe have some stuff that belonged to the twins? Like their pictures or something? It seems like every time I touched one of those, stuff got all kinds of paranormal," Clio said.

Ethan shrugged. "Sure. It can't hurt."

Clio stood up. She looked at the other faces around the table. "Could someone come with me? I'm a little scared to do it on my own."

"I'll help," Rebecca said. She walked over to the wall of portraits in the dining room. "Which one?" As her hands brushed the portrait of the Plunkett family, the lights flickered. Rebecca took a step backward. "Uh, I'm guessing it's this one?"

Clio nodded. "Be careful." Rebecca gently removed the picture from the wall. Wesley sat up, his ears erect. The crystal rattled softly in the china cabinet. Rebecca handed the old photo to Ethan and followed Clio to the front parlor.

The broken portrait of the twins lay flat on the coffee table. Rebecca looked at Clio expectantly. "This is the one that flew off the wall after I touched it. What if it happens again?" Clio asked.

"We can do it together, if you want," Rebecca said. Clio gingerly slipped her fingertips beneath the picture's edges, with Rebecca doing the same from the other side. As they lifted it up together, Clio felt a rush of cool air swirl through the room. A few of the piano keys tinkled softly.

The girls hurried back to the dining room, and Ethan placed the photos side by side on the table. "Now we just need to turn off all the lights in the house, and we'll be ready to go."

Maggie looked at Ethan. "*All* of them?"

Ethan nodded and opened the book, running his finger down a page in the middle. When the girls didn't move, he looked up. "What?"

"It's just, you know, a ghost in the house, weird stuff happening . . . maybe turning out all the lights isn't the best idea?" Rebecca said.

"Oh, don't worry about that," Ethan said. "Most ghosts are harmless, anyway."

"*Most* of them? Well, that's comforting," Maggie said sarcastically.

Tanya put down her pencil, picked up her phone, and tapped the flashlight app. "Come on. We can split up; it'll be faster that way."

Maggie grabbed her arm. "No splitting up! We go in pairs or not at all."

"But what about Ethan?" Rebecca asked. "Then he's left alone."

"Oh, I'm fine," Ethan said. "I'm alone all the time with ghosts. Besides, I've got company." He reached down and stroked Wesley, who stretched and rested his head on Ethan's foot.

The girls stood up, and Maggie linked her arm with Clio's. "We'll take the upstairs," she said. "Nothing spooky's ever happened up there," she whispered to Clio.

Clio and Maggie walked into the front hall. Just as they passed in front of the clock, it let out a booming chime, and Clio jumped. "Seriously!" She glared at it. "Creepy nasty garbage clock!"

Maggie checked the time on her phone. "It must

be broken. It's ten after nine; why would it chime now?" Clio looked at Maggie expectantly. "Oh, right," Maggie said. "Haunted house." She looked more closely at the clock. "It really *is* creepy." She reached out her hand to trace the strange carvings on its cabinet, but Clio stopped her.

"Don't touch it."

"Why not?"

"It just . . . doesn't like to be touched."

"Um, okay," Maggie said. She studied the clock. "Hey, look! You can see almost all of the moon lady." She pointed to the round, painted woman's face edging behind the clock's face. The eyes in the moon's face glimmered a soft yellow gold. "She looks kind of familiar."

"I know," Clio said, "but I can't place the face."

Maggie shrugged. "Me neither." The two girls walked upstairs. Maggie squeezed Clio's hand. "So do you think Ethan likes you?" she whispered.

"What?"

"I don't know. He seems kind of into you. He's all like, 'Oh, anything for Clio,' and stuff like that. Haven't you noticed?"

Clio switched off the light in the Lees' bedroom. "No."

Maggie led them farther down the hall. "Well, do you want him to? Like, do you *like* him?"

"Look, Ethan and I are just friends. Why are we even talking about this right now? In case you haven't noticed, we're kind of busy."

"Fine, okay. Sorry I asked. So you're just friends, then. Cool." The other upstairs rooms were closed and dark, but Maggie pointed at a bar of light coming from under the door across the hall from Minna's room. "Whose room is that?" Maggie asked.

"I don't know. It's always been locked, and I don't think the Lees have gotten around to clearing it out yet."

Just then, they heard a click and the door slowly opened a few inches. Maggie's face drained of color, her freckles stark against her bloodless cheeks. "Uhhh . . . you were saying?"

Clio looked at Maggie. She took a deep breath, steeling herself. "I guess it's unlocked after all. So now all we have to do is go in there and turn out the light."

"But do we, though?" Maggie asked.

Clio grabbed Maggie's hand. "Come on. We're in this together." She pushed open the door, and the two girls walked inside. It was a small room. The yellow wallpaper, peeling at the edges, was painted with a once-cheerful pattern of roses that had faded to a mousy gray. In the corner was a shelf of dusty books and antique toys. Across the room from a well-worn wardrobe, two sagging twin beds with carved headboards straddled a window hung with discolored lace curtains. Both beds were covered with quilts that were ragged with age and folded down to reveal a monogram stitched into the hem of each top sheet: HP and EP. In each bed, a china doll in a long, frilly dress with chipped, painted eyes sat up against the thin pillow at the headboard.

"This must have been the twins' room," Maggie whispered. "Do you think Harriet kept sleeping in the room after her sister died? Like, even as an old lady?"

"I don't know, but it feels really weird in here. Something obviously unlocked the door and turned the lamp on, right? So let's just turn it off and go back downstairs." Cautiously, the girls made their way across the room to switch off the old-fashioned lamp between the two beds. Clio looked back at the doorway. "Shoot. We should have turned on the hall light. I don't want to walk all the way back downstairs in the dark."

"I'll turn it on. Just a sec." Maggie stood in the doorway and peeked out. "It's on the other end of the hallway. Hang on. I'll be right back." She disappeared into the dark hall, leaving Clio alone in the room.

Clio walked a few steps closer to the beds and waited, ready to turn out the light as soon as Maggie got back. Where was Maggie? It should take only a second to flip on the light switch, and Maggie had been gone a lot longer than that. The room was hot, and Clio felt dizzy. She loosened her scarf and stepped forward, stumbling on the rug. She leaned on the nightstand to steady herself, closing her eyes. Her head ached.

Behind her, she heard the bedsprings groan on Eudora's bed. "Don't sit on there, Maggie," she said without turning around. There was a thump and

Eudora's doll fell to the floor, bumping her foot. "Be careful!" Clio said. She bent to pick up the doll and turned around.

There was no one there.

CHAPTER
20

THE LIGHT IN the hallway flicked on, and Maggie appeared in the doorway a moment later. "Did you call me?"

"Uh . . . no. But I'm pretty sure the ghost was in here with me. Let's just shut off the light and get back downstairs. I'll tell you on the way." Clio gently put the doll back on Eudora's bed, turned off the lamp, and hurried out of the room, closing the door firmly behind her.

The two girls walked quickly down the hallway, and Clio filled Maggie in on what had happened in the twins' room. The girls flipped the hall light off and picked their way down the creaking steps and through the dark first floor back to the dining room, where Ethan and the others sat at the table. Ethan had lit the candles, and their flickering flames cast wavering shadows that seemed to crawl across the walls and ceiling.

"Everything was quiet down here. Did you see anything upstairs?" Rebecca asked.

Maggie smiled grimly. "Oh, you know, just the usual stuff. We found the twins' bedroom, which was still all made up like a little girl's room, complete with toys, sheets, and everything. And then something invisible sat on Eudora's bed and dropped her doll. Just that kind of regular, normal stuff that people find when they go upstairs."

"Why do you think Eudora's haunting the house?" Rebecca asked. "All of her family is gone, so wouldn't she be at peace now that she's with them again?"

Ethan shrugged. "Sometimes something disruptive happens that can pull a spirit back into our world. It could be having a new family in the house, or the renovations the Lees are doing." He turned a page in the book on the table. "That's what we're here to find out."

"Do we have to hold hands, keep the circle unbroken, that sort of thing?" Maggie asked.

"Nah," Ethan said. "In the old days, people held hands to make sure someone wasn't cheating, pulling secret levers or knocking on the table or something. Believe it or not, there were a lot of frauds out there."

"Oh, I believe it," Tanya said.

"Who taught you all this, Ethan?" Rebecca asked.

Ethan blushed. "Nobody. The family gift was really strong back in the day, but since my mom's grandma, none of the family seems to have it. Or not that they would admit, anyway."

"So you're just kind of, like, figuring this out on your own? How do you know if you're doing it right?" Rebecca asked.

"It's kind of trial and error, I guess," Ethan said.

Rebecca smiled encouragingly. "Okay, so it's kind of like baking. The more I practiced, the better I got. My first soufflés were a disaster, but now they're little puffs of heaven. How many séances have you done before this one?"

Ethan scratched his head and looked down at the table. "Uh, this is actually my first."

Rebecca's smile fell. "Oh."

"Okay, that's enough questions." Clio's voice was impatient. "We've got to find Eudora's ghost and figure out how to send her back before the Lees get home on Monday, so let's get this show on the road."

Ethan picked up the bell and rang it once. "May we bring peace to all mortals and spirits who dwell in this house." He tied a thin cord to the bell's handle, hung it from the center of the chandelier, and sat back down. He looked at Clio, and she put the wooden mallet on the floor near the wall. Ethan closed his eyes. "Spirits, we invite you to speak with us tonight. You may ring this bell to answer yes to our questions and knock on the wall to answer no. Are there any spirits with us tonight who wish to make their presence known?"

Everyone stared at the bell expectantly. Clio held her breath. The seconds ticked by. Maggie fidgeted.

Then the bell rang softly.

"Did you hear that?" Clio whispered to Tanya.

Tanya nodded and wrote something down in her notebook.

Wesley whined and stood up, stiffly pacing the floor near Ethan's chair. He looked imploringly at Ethan. Ethan gently scratched the dog's bony side. "It's okay," Ethan whispered. "You can go." Wesley trotted from the room, and a few seconds later they heard the sound of his doggy door as the old dog pushed his way outside.

"Spirit," Ethan continued, "was this your home?" There was a pause, and the bell rang again.

"Are you here in this house because you miss your family?" Ethan asked. The bell rang over and over again, and the chandelier swayed.

"Be easy, spirit. Tonight our hope is to send you home to reunite you with your loved ones," Ethan said. The chandelier slowed, and the bell stopped ringing.

"Can I ask a question?" Clio whispered. Ethan nodded.

"Are you the ghost of Eudora Plunkett?" Clio looked expectantly at the bell. It was still. The girls looked at each other in confusion.

Suddenly, Clio heard a rap on the wall behind

her. The mallet's knocking grew louder. Soon unseen fists pounded on the walls. The ceiling shook. The china rattled in the cupboards. The table quaked, and Clio felt her chair move beneath her. Plaster dust fell from the ceiling like snow. Clio heard Wesley's doggy door flap in the kitchen, and the dishwasher door dropped open with a metallic crash. The piano keys pounded in the living room. "What's going on?!" Clio cried.

"I don't know!" Ethan frantically leafed through his book, but it flew from his hands and slammed against the opposite wall. The wooden chest of Moina's papers sprang open, and a storm of pages swirled about the room. The candles snuffed out.

The air was thick with plaster dust, the motes catching in the moonlight from the window. The chandelier swung with a vengeance. The bell cord snapped, and the bell fell to the table with a clatter. It rolled across the table's surface in tight, angry circles. Rebecca crawled under the table. "Come on! It's safer down here!"

Ethan and the girls cowered under the table as the room was engulfed in pandemonium. The chairs slid across the floor, banging into one another. "If we don't do something soon, this whole house is going to come falling down on our heads," Tanya yelled over the noise.

"Yeah, but what do we do?" Ethan asked.

"You're asking *me*?" Tanya replied incredulously. "I don't know! You're the expert!"

"I've never met a ghost like this!" Ethan shouted. "It seems pretty angry!"

Maggie snorted. "Thanks, Captain Obvious! So what do we do about it?"

"Find a way to make it . . . not angry?" Ethan asked uncertainly.

"That would be a good start!" Rebecca ducked as a book slammed into the edge of the table, barely missing her head.

The china cabinet on the wall groaned and began to rock. The chairs left the floor and floated around the table. "Somebody do something!" Maggie shrieked.

In desperation, Clio lifted her head and screamed. "Tell us what you want from us!"

The banging on the walls stopped. The swirling mass of papers and chairs dropped to the floor. Dust hung in the air.

The girls crawled out from under the table. Tanya switched on her flashlight and played the beam over the toppled furniture, torn papers, and fallen pictures. "Ethan, what happened?"

Ethan looked stricken. "I don't know."

The other girls switched on their flashlight apps and picked their way carefully through the rubble. Maggie rubbed her arms, which had broken out in goose bumps. "Is it over?"

Clio's flashlight beam lit up the wall. "No. It's definitely not over. Look at the mirror."

Blood red words covered the mirror: *SISTERS CAN NEVER BE PARTED.*

CHAPTER
21

"HARRIET," CLIO WHISPERED. Her legs were still trembling, and she put one hand on the table to steady herself.

"But . . . why?" Tanya asked, her voice hoarse. "Why would *Harriet's* ghost be haunting the house? She died an old lady."

Maggie forced a thin smile across her anxious face. "Ooh, you guys, did you hear that?" Maggie gave her friend's shoulders a squeeze. "I think Tanya finally just admitted ghosts are real!" She gestured around at the remnants of the evening's chaos. "I guess this little demonstration really won you over, huh?"

Tanya gritted her teeth and picked through the detritus on the floor, looking for her notebook.

"Is she still here?" Rebecca righted an upended chair and put it back in place at the dining table, her eyes darting nervously around the room.

Ethan swept up a pile of papers with his arms. "She's nearby."

"Why isn't she attacking us anymore?" Maggie asked. She opened the china cabinet to make sure nothing was broken.

"I think she wants us to help her," Ethan answered. "She wants to move on, but she's trapped here." He sorted through the pile of papers he had gathered.

Clio knelt down to help him. "What would keep her trapped here? Why do ghosts get stuck?" She took a handful of papers and stacked them neatly in the wooden chest.

Ethan smoothed out a crumpled piece of paper and handed it to Tanya. "Here, Tanya. I think this is from your notebook." He handed another stack of papers to Clio, and she flipped through them, turning them over so they all faced the same way. "Most spirits are happy to move on when they die, because it means they'll be reunited with their loved ones."

"But that doesn't make any sense," Tanya said. "Harriet spent her entire life trying to reunite with Eudora, right? So why stick around here if she could be with her sister instead?"

Clio looked down at the stack of papers she was sorting, and her eyes widened. "But what if she *couldn't* reunite with her sister? What if . . ." Clio struggled to formulate her thought into words. "What if when she died, she was expecting to see her sister again, only her sister wasn't there?"

"What do you mean? Where would she be?" Maggie asked.

"They never found Eudora's body, right?" Clio held up a child's drawing that was brown and brittle with age. "Look at this." The drawing showed a young girl and a tall woman in a long gown standing in the water, holding hands. The little girl had yellow hair with bangs. The tall woman had blue skin, and wild tendrils of hair stuck out from her head like spiders' legs.

"Eudora didn't drown in the pond. She was stolen by the Night Queen."

Rebecca, Maggie, Tanya, and Ethan stared at her in shock.

"That's why Harriet's still here!" Clio continued. "Her sister is trapped in the Nightmare Realm, and Harriet won't move on to the Spirit Realm without her. And if she drew that picture, she must have seen it happen."

"*Sisters can never be parted*," Rebecca whispered sadly. "Poor Harriet, to see her sister taken with no way to stop it."

"Poor Eudora!" Maggie said. "Imagine being trapped in the Nightmare Realm for over a hundred years. . . ." She shuddered, and the other girls grew quiet, remembering how close they had come to sharing Eudora's fate.

"We have to help them," Clio said. "We have to get Eudora back."

"But we can't get to the Nightmare Realm anymore, remember? We closed the portal. Besides, even if we could, the queen would never let us out of there alive," Maggie said. "Are you guys really willing to risk your lives for a couple of ghosts?"

Clio stood up. "But remember Minna's dream? Harriet's never going to leave this house without her sister, and you saw what she did in this dining room. If we don't help Harriet find Eudora, it's only going to get worse. The Lees will be in real danger. Especially Minna."

Maggie folded her arms. "I understand that, but I am not going back to the Nightmare Realm. I'm sorry, but I'm just not."

Clio looked at Ethan. "Maybe there's another way."

"What do you mean?" Rebecca asked.

"Well, we do have a spirit expert at our disposal," Clio said, gesturing to Ethan.

"Great idea." Tanya grinned at Clio. "So, how 'bout it, Ethan? Wanna help us rescue a spirit from the Nightmare Realm?"

Ethan blushed and took off his glasses, turning them over in his hands. "Uhh . . . I don't . . . no one's ever . . . I wasn't, um . . ." He polished the lenses with a corner of his shirt. "I, uh, wasn't . . . trained in that?" he finished lamely, his voice rising into a question.

"You weren't trained in any of this," Clio countered, "but you've done okay so far. Go with your gut."

Ethan thought for a moment. "Well, I don't know if it will work with the Nightmare Realm, but we could try making a spirit hole."

"A spirit hole?" Rebecca asked.

"Yeah. Sometimes there are places where the border between realms is thin. Thin enough to punch a hole in, allowing a spirit to slither through."

Maggie shivered. "Slithering spirits. Ugh."

Ethan shrugged. "Sorry. I don't know how else to describe it." He stood up. "I think I have all the stuff we need to do it. Let me go grab my ghost kit." He disappeared into the kitchen.

"Do you think it'll work?" Rebecca asked.

"It's worth a try, at least," Clio said. "Harriet and Eudora need our help, and whether they're ghosts or not, I'm not turning my back on them."

Tanya grabbed her pencil and opened to a fresh page in her notebook. She jotted down a few notes and looked up thoughtfully. "Wow, this whole realm thing is so fascinating! I mean, it just gives so much more support to the whole quantum multiverse theory, don't you think?"

"I have no idea what you just said," Maggie said, "but sure, definitely."

The girls laughed, and Clio stretched her arms over her head, easing some of the tension in her shoulders. "What's Ethan doing? I thought he was just getting his kit."

Then they heard the kitchen erupt in screams.

CHAPTER
22

"ETHAN!" MAGGIE SHOUTED. "Are you all right?"
The girls ran into the kitchen. Ethan was rolling
on the floor with a snarling, snapping creature,
both of them shrieking at the top of their lungs.
Ethan's glasses had been knocked off and lay
nearby.

Rebecca ran to the writhing pair and pulled
at the long, ropy arm that was wrapped around
Ethan's head. The creature looked up, startled.
"Horrible! What are you doing?" Rebecca cried.
"Get off him!"

The changeling's grip loosened, and Rebecca
dragged him away from Ethan, who was white with

fear, chest heaving. "What is that thing? I found it rummaging through my backpack."

"It's not a *thing*," Rebecca said huffily.

"That's the changeling I told you about," Clio explained.

Ethan looked in shock at Horrible, who sat placidly next to Rebecca, playing with a small mirror he had taken. A trickle of yellowish drool leaked from the corner of the changeling's gaping mouth. A few grubs wriggled out of his filthy blue onesie and dropped to the floor. "*That's* the changeling?" Ethan asked. "Wow. He is way uglier than you described." Horrible hissed and kicked at Ethan with his talons. "Wait, he can understand me?"

Rebecca nodded.

Maggie handed Ethan his glasses, keeping well out of the changeling's reach. "What's Horrible doing here, anyway?"

"That's a good question," Rebecca said. "Horrible, what are you doing here?"

The creature stood up, rocking slightly on his bowlegs. He scuttled across the kitchen floor and beckoned to Rebecca. When she didn't respond, he crept back to her and pulled at her wrist. She finally understood and let him lead her across the kitchen, the others following.

Horrible brought them past the pantry and into the hall, until they were standing in front of the clock. Hissing and cowering, the creature gesticulated at the clock. "What is it?" Rebecca asked. "I don't understand."

Horrible pointed at the clock's face. "Okay, so it's something to do with the clock," Tanya said, "but what *about* the clock?"

The changeling pointed more emphatically at the clock's face. "Do you want us to tell you what time it is?" Maggie asked impatiently. "Because don't bother with that thing. It's haunted and always wrong."

In frustration, Horrible jumped over to the window and pulled open the blinds, still clutching the mirror he had taken from Ethan's bag. Then he wriggled up the clock, grimacing as though he was in pain, and sat at the top, his talons digging into the wood. "Be careful of the wood!" Rebecca said.

Horrible ignored her. He dug his claws in deeper and pointed at the clock's face. A shaft of moonlight shone through the window, and Horrible caught the silvery beam in the mirror's glass, aiming it at the clock's face. As soon as the light hit the woman on the clock, she transformed. Spider legs sprouted from her head, and her skin turned a deep, midnight blue.

"That's no moon!" Clio gasped. "It's the Night Queen."

The group stood staring at the clock for a moment, stunned. Finally, Maggie spoke. "No wonder that clock is so awful!"

Tanya wrote frantically in her notebook. "Why is he showing us this?"

"I don't know," Rebecca answered, "but he obviously wants to keep the Night Queen out of our world just as much as we do. I think that's why he followed us to the portal that night, to make sure it was really closed and she couldn't come after him." She looked at the changeling with sympathy. "Maybe he's been hanging around here for the same reason. If this thing adds to her power, then it has to be shut down, and I don't think Horrible could do that alone."

"So he's on our side?" Tanya asked dubiously.

"Does it matter?" Maggie said. "As long as he's helping us defeat *her*, I'll take it!"

Horrible hopped down from the clock and clawed at its cabinet door, his mushroom-tipped fingers scrabbling ineffectively at the glass.

"It's okay," Clio said. "I got it." She pulled on the cabinet's handle. As soon as her fingers touched the clock, the bells inside slammed together with a deafening clang that rang on and on. Clio tried to jump back, but Horrible pushed her forward. "What is it?" she shouted over the ringing. The others covered their ears at the unbearable sound.

Horrible pointed down inside the clock. Clio reached her arm down, feeling around the rough wooden sides. A splinter sliced into her finger. "Ouch!" She tried to pull her hand back, but Horrible hopped frantically up and down, urging her on. She pushed her arm down still farther, as far as she could reach, until her fingers just grazed the bottom. She ran her hand along the cabinet floor until her fingers closed on something light and thin. She pulled it out, and the chiming ceased.

The clock's ticking wheezed and faltered before stopping entirely.

Clio held up the slender white object, drops of blood oozing from her finger. "I'm guessing this is what you wanted me to find?" Horrible hopped up and down.

The others crowded around. Maggie took it from Clio's hand and held it closer to the light. "What is it?"

Tanya peered closer. "Uh, it looks like a finger bone."

"OMG, ew!" Maggie dropped the bone on the floor and jumped away.

Ethan picked it up and closed his eyes. He breathed in and out slowly, then opened his eyes. "It's Harriet's," he said. "And I think I can use it to find her sister."

CHAPTER 23

ETHAN HELD THE bone in the palm of his hand. "Have you guys heard of dowsing?"

Tanya laughed. "Have I ever! It's one of the biggest scams of the Middle Ages. People had forked sticks that they claimed magically helped them find underground water." She shook her head and snorted. "Honestly, people back then would believe almost anything!"

Ethan blushed. "Um, yeah. So, uh, my dad is descended from a British clan of dowsers that dates back to the 1400s. That's how we got our last name." He shrugged. "You know. Underwood: *Under*ground water found with *wood*."

"Oh. That's neat," Tanya said faintly, her face a mask of embarrassment. "Yeah. Sorry about that. I'm sure your ancestors were really great dowsers. Totally legit."

Ethan grinned at the floor and shook his head. "Don't worry about it." He picked up the bone with his other hand, holding it between his forefinger and thumb. "We can use this to do something called spirit dowsing." He closed his eyes, and the bone twitched lightly in his fingers. "In spirit dowsing, the bone works like a divining rod, only instead of guiding us to water, it guides us to the trapped spirit." He opened his eyes.

"That's so cool," Rebecca said. "Do you think it will really work?"

The bone twitched again in Ethan's fingers. "Well, usually we need a bone from the spirit's own body, but Harriet and Eudora were as close as two people could be, and this bone seems to be itching to lead us somewhere."

A cool breeze blew through the hallway, lifting Clio's scarf for a moment before it gently fluttered down again. "I think Harriet approves," Clio said.

Ethan smiled at Clio. "Looks like I may not be

the only one who has a talent for understanding ghosts."

Following the bone like a compass, Ethan led the others out the back door. Horrible scampered behind them for a moment before disappearing into the woods. "So much for being on our side," Tanya said.

"Oh, leave him alone," Rebecca said. "He's scared. I mean, would you hang around here if you didn't have to?"

"No way," Maggie said. "Do you think it's too late for me to go with him?" Clio laughed and gave her friend a squeeze.

The night was quiet and cool, and the light from the moon edged the tree line with silver. A shadow detached itself from the darkness of the garage and loped over to join them. "Hey, buddy," Ethan said to the dog. Wesley nuzzled the boy's palm and leaned into him. "It's safe for the time being, but it could get a little hairy later, so you may want to lie low." Wesley licked Ethan's hand and trotted off back to the garage.

The kids soon found themselves near the pond, and Ethan stopped. Past the pond they could just make out the crumbling pillars of the folly, its interior cloaked in shadow. "She's in the pond," Maggie whispered, but Ethan shook his head. Maggie gave him a quizzical look. "But she has to be in the pond, doesn't she? It's where she disappeared."

"It's where she was last seen," Clio said, "but I don't think it's where the Night Queen took her." She looked at Ethan. "Am I right?"

Ethan nodded approvingly. "You're really good at this, you know?" He pointed at the folly. "I think we can find her in there."

Tanya offered her flashlight to Rebecca. "Can you hold this? I want to take notes." Rebecca grinned and held out her hand. She clicked on the switch and shone the light into the dark recesses of the folly. The dim light barely penetrated the deep shadows, and the group gingerly crept forward.

Even though the structure had no walls, the air felt immediately dank once they crossed the threshold. The smell of pungent decay hung over everything, and the folly's pitted marble floor was slick with moss. Clio tread carefully behind Ethan.

"Ugh. This place is so . . . Night Queen–y," Maggie mumbled. "I can't believe Butch would have taken anyone on a date here!" She slipped on the moss and grabbed onto Rebecca for support. "At least Bad Breath Stanley took her someplace nice."

A marble fountain stood at the center of the folly. The finger bone vibrated in Ethan's hand, leading him straight to it.

"Rebecca, can you shine the flashlight on that?" Tanya asked, nodding toward the fountain. She lifted up her pencil to make a sketch.

Rebecca ran the beam up the base until it shone on the fountain's marble statue. It was a woman leading a little girl by the hand, guiding her into the fountain's basin. The woman's feet had disappeared into the pool, and her long gown was carved to look as though it were floating on the surface. The little girl's bare toe was just dipping below the waterline. Choked with algae, the fountain's water burbled thickly into the catch pool below.

Tanya's pencil stopped sketching. "It's Harriet's drawing," she breathed. "This is where Eudora disappeared."

CHAPTER 24

THE GIRLS STARED in wonder at the statue. The woman's face had weathered away, but they could still make out the faint spidery shape of her hair and the delicate curve of her ram's horn crown. "Harriet must have had this fountain built after her parents died," Clio said. "She never wanted to forget what happened to her sister."

Ethan rummaged through his kit and pulled out a few items, which he piled on the slippery floor near the fountain's edge. Finally, he looked up. "Okay, I think I've got it all." He picked up the bone and worked his way around the fountain's base. After a few moments, he stopped in front of a blackened marble tile that poked out from the floor like a decayed tooth. "It's here."

The girls rushed over. Ethan placed a marble mortar and pestle in front of the stone. He unscrewed a small jar and scooped a few spoonfuls of loamy material into the mortar. "What is that?" Rebecca asked.

"Soil from a fresh grave," Ethan answered. "It represents the physical link between life and death." He opened another small jar and poured some liquid into the mortar. "Now I'm adding mourners' tears. That represents the spiritual link." He ground the two together. "So I mix them together and make—"

"Mud!" Maggie interjected. She noticed the deadpan looks on the others' faces. "Sorry, just trying to lighten the mood. Jeez."

Ethan dipped his fingers into the mixture and daubed the paste onto the stone. "Do you want to help?" Clio knelt down and dipped her fingers into the mortar. The muddy paste was gritty and cool, and her fingertips tingled where it touched her. Following Ethan's lead, she daubed the paste and began spreading it in a thin layer over the stone. The other girls joined in, and when the marble tile was completely covered, Ethan stopped them. "We have to spread the spirit paste with our bare hands, but make sure you go to the pond and rinse all of it off before we open the spirit hole. This stuff works as a kind of conductor, so we definitely don't want it anywhere it shouldn't be."

The pond was covered with a thin layer of scum. Clio grimaced when she dipped her hands in. The slime seemed to cling to her skin. Beside her, Ethan scrubbed out the mortar and pestle, drying his hands on the grass.

"I wish I had brought my backpack down here," Rebecca said. "We could be smelling like cotton candy–scented wipes instead of stanky pond scum."

"Seriously!" Maggie said. "This is a one-way ticket to barftown!" She gingerly dipped her fingers in and snatched them away as soon as they touched the algae-choked surface.

Back at the fountain, Ethan knelt on the ground near the stone. He looked around at the others. "Are you ready?"

Rebecca tentatively raised her hand. "Just out of curiosity, how many times have you done this before?"

"Um, yeah. Never," Ethan answered.

Rebecca sighed. "I figured."

Ethan placed the bone on the stone tile. "Harriet's bone should work like a magnet, drawing Eudora back to us." He opened a tiny jar filled with glittering particles.

"What's that?" Tanya asked.

"Gold dust," Ethan said. "Iron creates barriers; gold opens them."

Tanya nodded and bent over her notebook. "Interesting," she muttered to herself. "Both elements."

Ethan sprinkled a tiny amount of gold dust onto the bone. "Here we go," he said. The girls bent closer, crowding in to see what would happen.

A delicate wisp of dark smoke curled up from the stone, and Ethan and the girls pressed forward eagerly. The smoke dissipated, and the stone looked the same as before. "Aw, man," Maggie said. "That was lame." Just then, a sliver of cold silver made a tiny opening in the stone, forming a pinpoint of light on the domed ceiling of the folly.

"It's working!" Clio said. The hole in the stone

grew larger. Wind blew through the folly, scattering dead leaves across the cracked marble floor. From out of the opening came a pale, twisting wraith that stretched and curled like a ribbon, twining searchingly around each of the girls. It touched Clio with an icy cold tendril, and she could smell the faint scent of roses.

"Is that Eudora?" Rebecca whispered. "What's she doing?"

"I think she's looking for Harriet," Clio whispered back. The wraith weaved itself around the statue and up to the ceiling, moving as fluidly as a jellyfish. Clio watched it, entranced. "I never thought it would be so beautiful," she said softly.

Ethan grinned. "Nobody ever does."

Rebecca cleared her throat and pointed at the spirit hole. "Uh, is that supposed to happen?" The hole had widened, and the light beaming out of it had turned from a serene silver to an ominous dark gray. The light seemed almost alive, forming itself into tentacles that reached out searchingly. The kids recoiled, scuttling backward to get out of the light's reach.

"Hey, Ethan, anytime you want to close that spirit hole would probably be a good idea," Tanya said.

Ethan frantically flipped through the pages of his book. "I'm working on it. I just have to figure out how." The dark light slithered from the hole, the thin streams crawling across the ground like snakes.

"Wait, you opened a spirit hole you don't know how to close?" Tanya asked, her voice tight with tension.

"We were in a rush!" Ethan shot back. "You're the ones who told me to go with my gut!"

"You guys! A little less arguing and a little more spirit-hole-closing, if you don't mind? This thing is starting to look pretty nasty." Maggie pointed at the twisting tendrils that stretched almost to her feet.

"Maggie!" Rebecca shouted. "What's wrong with you?" Maggie's fingers were a glowing silver, and so was a spot on her leopard-print leggings. The glowing spots acted as beacons, pulling the dark tentacles to her.

"There must be spirit paste on her!" Ethan

cried. "It's drawing the Nightmare Realm straight to her!"

"I—I didn't want to wash my hands in the gross pond water!" Maggie exclaimed.

"So you wiped your ghost-summoning mud hands on your *leggings?*" Rebecca asked incredulously.

The hole widened, and a skeletal, rotting arm punched through and reached blindly for Maggie. "It's a lusus!" Tanya shouted. She lunged forward and whacked at the arm with her notebook. A second arm burst through the spirit hole with a crunching sound. Skeletal fingers stretched out, the bony fingertips just grazing Maggie's toe. Maggie kicked it away and tried to scramble backward, but the glowing spots held her in place.

"Help me!" Maggie cried. The rotting hand closed tightly around her ankle, and Maggie screamed as it dragged her closer to the hole. Tanya kicked and punched at the arm, but her blows were no match for the lusus's sinewy strength.

The second arm swiped at Maggie's other foot, and Rebecca grabbed a loose chunk of marble and slammed it down on the bony fingers. Two of the

fingers broke into splinters that wriggled on the stone like beached fish, but the hand kept reaching for Maggie.

Maggie clawed at the slippery marble tile as the arm pulled her almost to the hole's edge. She kicked at the arm with her free foot, trying desperately to break its hold. The other hand clamped onto her shoe, and the toe of her sneaker disappeared into the hole. "They're going to pull her in!" Clio shouted. She ran over to Maggie and grabbed her under the arms, pulling against the lusus with all her might. Maggie screamed as she was stretched between the lusus and her friends. "Ethan!" Clio cried. "We have to close it!"

"I'm trying!" Ethan leafed through his book and pulled jars out of his backpack, scanning the label of each before tossing it aside.

Tanya and Rebecca beat against the lusus's arms, and Clio pulled with as much strength as she could muster, but it wasn't enough. Maggie was being drawn steadily deeper into the spirit hole.

CHAPTER 25

"ETHAN!" CLIO CRIED. "Come help me! I can't hold her much longer!" Ethan jumped up and grabbed Maggie's hands. They dug in their heels and pulled. Maggie shrieked as one leg disappeared farther into the hole. "Rebecca! Tanya! We're going to lose her! Grab hold!"

The other girls grabbed onto her legs, trying to find traction on the slippery, moss-covered tiles. "Don't let me go!" Maggie begged, tears streaming down her face.

Clio gritted her teeth. "If you go, we all go." She felt her heels skid across the stones as the whole group was dragged closer.

Rebecca kicked at the arms, and her blue suede sneaker slipped off her foot and disappeared into the hole. "We're not going to make it!"

"Don't give up yet!" Clio locked her legs under Maggie's arms and used her free hand to scrabble for Ethan's kit.

"What are you doing?" Tanya shouted.

"Looking for the iron!"

"The what?"

Clio tipped the bag over, scattering bottles everywhere. "Gold opens, iron closes, remember?" She grabbed a bottle of red powder and smashed it open on the arms grabbing Maggie. There was a flash like a lightning bolt, and the arms disappeared down the hole, breaking their hold. The hole began to shrink, and the group scrambled backward. The wraith circled anxiously above, twisting around the fountain statue like a cat.

Just as the hole was about to close completely, a rotting arm burst back through and gripped the hole's edge, pushing against it. A shoulder emerged as a lusus tried to force its way through before the opening could seal. "It's blocking the hole so it can't close!" Tanya cried.

"We need something to destroy the lusus!" Ethan shouted. Tanya scrabbled through the jars and tossed them to Ethan. He unscrewed the lid of one and flung the contents onto the emerging lusus. It sizzled when it touched the creature's skin, but the monster kept coming.

"It's not working!" Clio picked up a chunk of marble and hurled it at the lusus. She looked up at the ghost. "Eudora, help us!"

Above them the wraith tugged at the fountain's statue, rocking it against the foundation. Stone scraped and water sloshed over the sides of the catch basin, but the fountain stayed secure.

"What is she doing?" Rebecca cried.

The lusus's head was just emerging through the edge of the hole. Red, swollen eyes seeped black liquid down its sunken face, and its broken teeth were sharp and jagged.

Just then, a second wraith flew from the direction of the house. It joined the first, wrapping itself around the statue. The statue rocked harder, and water splashed against the pavement, soaking the girls' and Ethan's feet.

With a final shriek of stone on stone, the statue

teetered forward and toppled. The heavy marble collapsed onto the lusus, crushing the creature into a fine black powder. The dark light faded away, and a cloud of marble dust filled the air. When it cleared, the spirit hole was gone.

Above them, the two wraiths twined around each other. A gentle breeze lifted the hair from Clio's neck, and the faint scent of roses permeated the air. "Thank you for saving us," Clio whispered. She felt the cool touch of the wraiths' fingers stroking her cheek before the spirits swooped out of the folly and pooled like a fog on the dew-covered grass. The fog formed into the image of two little girls. Clio could just make out the outline of their matching white dresses and the bows in their hair. Hand in hand, the spirits drifted across the lawn and disappeared quietly into the pond.

Harriet and Eudora were finally going home.

CHAPTER 26

WESLEY WAS WAITING at the back door when Clio and her friends returned to the house. Ethan stroked the hound's shaggy head. Horrible was nowhere to be seen. "It figures that little monster took off when we could have used his help the most," Maggie grumbled as they walked into the kitchen.

"You can't hold that against him," Rebecca said. "Remember what happened to him the last time he was anywhere near the Nightmare Realm? He served and trusted the Night Queen, and she almost turned him to ashes."

"Besides, he helped us find the bone and shut down that awful clock." Clio walked into the front hall and stood in front of the grandfather clock. It was silent now, and she was amazed at how much more at ease she felt without its incessant ticking.

"What is the deal with this thing, anyway?" Tanya asked, running her hands over the wood. "Was it another portal?"

Clio shook her head. "I felt all around the inside, and there was no opening. I don't know what it was for, but whatever it is, it won't work now."

The group finished clearing up the dining room. "It's a miracle nothing was broken," Rebecca remarked as she hung the last picture back on the wall.

"Tell me about it," Ethan said. "I'd hate to be fired from my first dogsitting gig at the Lees' for trashing their house."

Ethan and the girls took one last look around, making sure everything was put away and settled before Clio texted her aunt to pick them up. Upstairs in the twins' bedroom, Clio noticed the two dolls were no longer displayed on separate beds. Instead, they sat side by side on Eudora's bed. Clio smiled and closed the bedroom door.

As she finished her final walk-through of the

rooms, Clio noticed a lightness in the air that she hadn't felt before. It was as though the dark cloud that had always hung over the house had finally faded away. She closed the front door behind her and joined her friends on the front porch. Rebecca touched her shoulder. "Everything okay?" Kawanna's headlights lit up the yard as she pulled into the driveway.

Clio nodded. "I think the Lees are going to be very happy here."

. . . . .

Kawanna had just turned the CLOSED sign on the shop's front door when Clio and her friends arrived the following evening. "Just in time," Kawanna said. "I haven't had a moment to sit down all day!"

"I'll make the tea this time," Rebecca offered, and disappeared down the hall to the tiny apartment behind the shop. Kawanna flopped onto the sagging leather armchair in her office, and the girls squeezed in on the loveseat. Ethan perched on the arm.

Rebecca came back with the silver tea tray and passed around cups of herbal tea. She held up hers for a toast. "Here's to the end of another supernatural adventure. May it be our last!" The others laughed and clinked their cups together for the toast.

Ethan sipped shyly from his cup. "Thanks for inviting me," he said.

"Are you kidding? We couldn't have done it without you!" Tanya said.

Maggie gave Ethan a playful nudge with her foot. "Did you hear that? Sounds like you finally won her over!" She leaned in closer, lowering her voice. "And believe me, that's not easy to do."

"I heard that!" Tanya said, and threw her balled-up napkin at Maggie.

"What's the news on the fellowship project?" Kawanna asked Clio. "It was due today, wasn't it?"

"I turned it in first thing this morning," Clio answered.

"Nice!" Kawanna high-fived her niece.

"I bet your project was amazing," Ethan said. "I just know you're going to get it!"

The room grew quiet as everyone sipped their tea. "Last night was a pretty close call," Clio said softly. She rested her head on Kawanna's shoulder.

Kawanna stroked her niece's hair. "But you made it through," she said. "You looked out for each other, and you kept your heads. I couldn't be prouder of all of you."

Maggie squeezed Clio's hand. "And don't forget Harriet and Eudora, Clio. Those girls waited more than a century for someone to come along and help them, and you're the one who did it. I saw how scared you were, but you didn't let that stop you. You didn't let it stop you from saving me, either." She looked at the ground shyly. "Any of you. You guys saved my life."

Tanya put her arm around Maggie and gave her a squeeze. "We never would have let you go. No matter what. That's what friends do."

· · · · ·

Mrs. Lee waved as the junk haulers pulled out of the driveway. She turned to her husband. "It's a shame we had to get rid of that old clock. It was such a beautiful piece. Maybe we should have tried harder to have it fixed."

Mr. Lee smiled at his wife. "Don't worry. We'll find something new. We have a lifetime together to fill this house with beautiful pieces." He looked down at his daughter. "Isn't that right, Minna?"

Minna hugged her father's legs and ran into the

kitchen. She came back with Wesley following behind, his skinny tail wagging. Minna held up a painting of a bright blue lumpy blob. "We could hang this up!"

Her parents smiled at each other over her head. "I think that's just perfect," Mr. Lee said, and tacked it to the wall.

Mrs. Lee handed Minna a pen and picked her up. "Every artist has to sign her work," she said. Minna carefully printed her name in the corner of the painting.

"That makes it official," Mr. Lee said. "Our first piece in the Lee family art collection!"

The family's laughter could be heard through the open windows as the last rays of the setting sun slipped past the house and spread across the pond, bathing it with gold. The water was tranquil and clear, the secrets beneath its surface finally at peace.

EPILOGUE

THE FULL MOON rose over the mounds of the dump, casting in stark silhouette the rusting refrigerators, broken chairs, and occasional raccoon scavenging for a free meal. Near the top of one pile, a grandfather clock rose up at an odd angle like a crooked tombstone. The clock was streaked with grime, its walnut cabinet gouged and chipped from the weeks it had spent in the elements. A midnight-blue woman's face peered from behind the tarnished silver faceplate, the hands frozen in place, eternally 11:59. A family of rats sniffed at the cabinet, searching in vain for a forgotten crumb.

Silver moonlight spilled across the clock's surface, and the minute hand shot forward to meet the hour hand. The rats scattered.

In heavy, sonorous tones, the clock began to chime.

Acknowledgments

I turned this book in a week before we left Los Angeles to begin a new adventure in Minneapolis. I do not recommend moving while on deadline, and I am very grateful for the many people who helped me keep my misery to a minimum. First and foremost, thanks especially to my mom for all the phone calls and words of encouragement as I frantically tried to get everything done. And to the Fanuele family, who did everything from stocking our fridge to lending us their car, thank you for making our adopted city feel like home from the very first moment. As always, big love to my infinitely wise and patient agent, Erin Murphy, and to everyone in the EMLA family for your ongoing kindness and support. To my editor, Erin Stein, and to Natalie Sousa, Nicole Otto, Kelsey Marrujo, and the whole Imprint team, thank you for your continued work with me to bring this series to readers. Seeing kids' excitement about these books is pretty much the greatest feeling ever. And Rayanne Vieira, you absolutely nailed this one; hearts came out of my eyes when I saw the cover. Kirsten Cappy and Curious City continue to amaze and inspire me with new ways to connect to readers, and I can't say enough great things about Jenny Medford and Websy Daisy for the beautiful babysittingnightmares.com website.

To all the teachers, librarians, and fellow authors who have so warmly embraced this series, you have my deepest admiration and gratitude. Thank you for all you do to champion books and promote joyful literacy. Eternal thanks to Elly Swartz, who continues to be an incredible inspiration and a cherished friend. I couldn't have done any of this without you. Special thanks to Jarrett Lerner and Jennifer Chambliss-Bertman for your support and wonderful words of encouragement. Much love also to Angela Whited and Lily Tschudi-Campbell at Red Balloon Bookshop in St. Paul for your boldly bookish awesomeness. Huge hugs to Debbi Michiko-Florence and Sarah Azibo for the e-mails and phone calls, especially in those times when I was feeling really stuck and lost. Kathi and Jeffrey, Sharon and Adam, Tiffany, Julie, Jessica, Joeanna, Lara, Anne and Chris, Barky, and Alex at the Copper Still made it really hard to leave Los Angeles, as did Robin Savoian and all the folks at the LA Zoo. And to the powerful ladies of LA LAW, how I adore, admire, and miss each and every one of you. To the Sheps/Knudys, the Gam Fam, and the Hubens, I'm so lucky to have you in my cheering section. And I reserve my deepest gratitude for my very best and favorite, Eddie Gamarra. It is always for you, my love.

About the Author

KAT SHEPHERD loves to create fast-paced adventure stories that are likely to engage reluctant readers because she wholeheartedly believes that reading should be a joyful experience for every child.

A former classroom teacher, Kat has also spent various points in her life working as a deli waitress, a Hollywood script reader, and a dog trainer for film and TV. She lives in Minneapolis with her husband, two dogs, and a rotating series of foster dogs. Babysitting Nightmares is her first middle grade series.

katshepherd.com

babysittingnightmares.com